Traveling for Love
Searching for Self, Hoping for Love

by

Becky Due

TELEMACHUS
PRESS

This book is a work of fiction. Names, characters, places and incidents are either the product of the author's imagination or are used fictitiously. Any resemblance to actual persons, living or dead, or to actual events or locales is entirely coincidental.

TRAVELING FOR LOVE: SEARCHING FOR SELF, HOPING FOR LOVE

Cover design by Andreea Barbulescu

Published by Telemachus Press, LLC
http://www.telemachuspress.com

ISBN# 978-1-937698-16-4 (eBook)
ISBN# 978-1-937698-17-1 (Paperback)

Version 2014.01.07

Printed in the United States of America

10 9 8 7 6 5 4 3 2 1

Traveling for Love
Searching for Self, Hoping for Love

Chapter 1

"YOU'RE A MISERABLE person. I don't even know who you are," he had said to me. He was right. I am miserable, and I don't know who I am. I stared out the living room window trying to figure out how I lost myself in these fourteen years of marriage. Tears rolled down my cheeks.

Nick left town to avoid the drama of me packing and moving out. I volunteered to leave because I couldn't afford the house anyway. My friend Teresa said she'd love to have me live with her, so that's where I was headed.

I couldn't believe I was leaving my home. As I watched the cars drive by, I hoped his car would pull into the driveway and he'd rush in and tell me how sorry he was and how much he loved me and he'd beg me to stay. The cars just kept passing by.

Then a big yellow school bus full of children drove by.

Feelings of failure flooded over me as I stood up to finish packing. I took many breaks in my favorite chair to look out the window and cry over memories. I was still in shock over what was really happening—*we are getting a divorce.*

I should have realized there was a problem when I started researching getting a facelift. People kept saying things to me like, "You look tired." or "Are you feeling okay?" Even Nick kept asking me, "What's wrong?" or "You look so sad." I just assumed my face was sagging and I needed a facelift; it never occurred to me that I was tired, I was not feeling well and I was deeply sad. I had also noticed that I didn't stand up straight, and my shoulders seemed to slouch forward. I felt old, run down.

As I walked into each room to sort through my things, my wedding ring felt heavy on my finger, but I wasn't ready to take it off. *You're a miserable person. I don't even know who you are,* kept replaying in my mind and the tears blurred my eyes while I pulled shoes out of the closet by the front door. Then I saw my rollerskates.

When I was young, I used to love to roller-skate. So about a year ago, I tried to pick it up again. I ordered these beautiful white skates with red wheels and red laces. I was so excited when they arrived. Skating was my attempt to find myself again. The day they were delivered, I laced them up and took off down our long driveway. I was happy; I felt like a fearless teenager without a care in the world. The driveway was more sloped than I had realized and I was gaining speed. I didn't remember how to slow down, so I quickly turned backwards to use my toe breaks to stop but I was going too fast and I fell hard on my hip and arm. The pavement scrapped the skin off my arm, side and butt and I was bleeding like crazy. I took off my skates and walked stocking foot back to the house. I never put the skates on again. I rolled them out of the closet but couldn't decide if I should pack them or leave them behind.

I sat down by the window and imagined myself skating down the driveway and falling. I knew what that fall did to me. I lost another small part of who I was. I wondered if I would ever get the happy me back, if I would ever find her again.

It wasn't Nick's fault, I did it to myself. I let myself go. I stopped liking myself. But I did like Nick; for some crazy reason, I liked Nick. *Please drive up the driveway. Please drive up the driveway!*

Am I really that awful?

"You'll find somebody who likes to do the things you like, what-ever that is," he had said to me.

I went upstairs to take a shower, and sat by the drain on the tile floor crying until the hot water turned cold. "Who am I? Who am I?" I cried.

The long shower and hard cry helped. I realized that although I didn't know who I was or what exactly I liked, I knew what I didn't like. This gave me hope that by the process of elimination, I could find out who I was.

I knew I didn't like the same things Nick liked, but yet, I did almost everything he wanted to do. The last year or two I cut back on doing what Nick wanted, so he had to go with friends or alone. I didn't even feel guilty about it anymore. I was glad when he left to do something without me. I felt off the hook and free for a couple of hours.

I was worn out from doing things that, if I were single, I would never want to do. When we met, he didn't smoke, but he'd picked up the habit again, and I found myself married to a smoker, a habit I despised.

Nick bought a motorcycle, then expected me to ride with him even though he knew how much I disliked motorcycles. My old boy-friend had had a terrible accident on his motorcycle and I'd hated them ever since, and yet there I was, hopping on the back of his bike every time he wanted me to.

Nick liked country music and wanted to go to country music concerts. I didn't like country. I didn't like Vegas or gambling either, but every time he wanted to go, I went. He loved to be outside, but only to lie in the sun. I didn't mind occasionally lying in the sun but for the most part, if I was going to be outside, I wanted to be active, playing catch, going for walks or swimming laps, not just lying there doing nothing. I was bored and annoyed every time he wanted to lie in the sun with me.

"I'd like to get you a bike so you can ride it while I run. I know you can't run with me because of your bad feet, but you could ride with me. That might be fun," I'd say, and he'd follow with, "You get yourself a bike; it sounds like something you'd enjoy."

"I'd like to go to a concert coming up. Will you go with me?" I'd ask, and he's say, "I have a better idea. Why don't you find a friend to go with you?"

"Let's take a weekend road trip and go someplace we've never gone!" I'd suggest and he'd say, "You know I can't stand to be in the car that long."

Our whole marriage was like that. I went his way but he didn't come my way. And maybe it was my own fault because I didn't force him to meet me half way.

I walked into the kitchen and stood in front of the refrigerator. The tears came back when I saw the fridge stocked full of Nick's favorite bottled water, favorite pop and favorite beer. There was just enough room for two bottles of my favorite sparkling water on the door shelf. Each time I took one, I had to remember to replace it with one from the pantry. He said there wasn't enough room, and because he made most of the money in our marriage, the fridge should be stocked with his favorite drinks.

I had convinced myself he was right. He made most of the money, so he dictated what we did, he chose what we watched on TV, he decided where and how we vacationed. Nick's idea of travel was staying at a different hotel every time we went to Las Vegas. My vacations came whenever he went out of town without me—the TV was always on the Travel Channel or one of the health and fitness channels. I took better care of myself whenever he was gone, and I liked myself more. I pulled a bottle of my sparkling water from the door and didn't bother replacing it with a warm one from the pantry.

The phone rang, startling me. I checked caller ID and saw it was Teresa. "Well, Amanda, your room is cleaned out and ready for you. Hurry up and get here. We are going to have so much fun!"

I wasn't scheduled to start sleeping there for a couple more days—when Nick came back—but I could tell she was trying to give me something to look forward to and her enthusiasm helped. Teresa and I had been friends for a long time. We weren't close, but she had just gotten a divorce and she was looking for a roommate. The thought of having a roommate at forty years old was unsettling, but in some ways exciting. She was in a partying mood, trying to recapture her twenties that she missed out on because she was married. And in some ways I wanted to let loose a little, drink and party.

Teresa kept telling me that I needed a nice quick rebound, but I wasn't sure. I wanted to keep the door open with Nick just in case he missed me. Maybe he could change. Maybe I could change.

The thought of having sex with somebody besides Nick was somewhat thrilling. I was faithful to Nick but often felt lonely, sometimes even wishing for an affair. I wanted to be rescued from Nick, and I thought a man could save me.

Our sex life had fizzled out, too. For the entire fifteen years we were together, I asked him to do one simple thing while we made love: I wanted him to keep his hands on my breasts because it was the key to my orgasms, but he refused. I'd beat myself up, not understanding why he couldn't do that for me. I just assumed my breasts were too small for his liking, not worth holding on to. And I guess neither was I.

Chapter 2

I HAD BEEN living with Teresa for six months and working full-time at the travel agency. My coworkers and I often went to a deli down the block from where we worked. Sam's seriousness and his indifference to me made him even more attractive. He wasn't a flirt or a jokester like one of the other deli workers who tried to get every female customer's attention. Sam was different. He didn't want attention, even though I tried to get his. He didn't look at anybody; he didn't look at my friends and he didn't look at me.

Sam always seemed a little sad and so did I, maybe that's why I was drawn to him. He appeared older, but I was sure he was younger than me. He was a big man—six four, maybe taller—and well built. He wasn't the most attractive man I'd ever seen but something about him intrigued me. He had a strong masculine face and he never smiled. He was all about business: taking the order, making the sandwich, collecting the money, wiping down the counters, cleaning the tables, mopping the floor.

For weeks, I watched him from a distance. I wondered what his story was: *Maybe he is married or has a girlfriend and he's miserable the way I was. Maybe he hates his job. Maybe he is one of those extremely introverted people. Maybe he is hiding from the law or in that witness protection program. Or maybe he just wants to be left alone.*

After several failed attempts to get him to smile or at least acknowledge me, I gave up. I was sick of sandwiches anyway and couldn't afford to continue eating out with my friends, so I started packing my own lunch and eating at my desk. I usually finished eating in about fifteen minutes, so I'd spend the rest of my lunch hour walking around downtown before heading to Starbucks for my afternoon fix—a tall raspberry mocha. And I always secretly hoped I'd run into Sam on the street and he'd notice me, maybe even talk to me.

Weeks passed and I had forgotten about Sam and the deli—I didn't have time for crushes. I was forty, newly divorced and childless, so I returned to my original focus of saving money and daydreaming about traveling to beautiful, exotic places. Working at the travel agency was motivating, but frustrating because I was stuck behind my desk while planning perfect trips for others. But by packing my own lunch and limiting my outings with friends, I hoped one day to be one of those travelers.

One weekend night when I was planning to stay in, my roommate, Teresa said, "Let's go dancing!" then added, "You'll burn calories. Not so easy to keep the weight off after forty," she teased. Teresa, newly divorced at forty-one, was determined to be remarried before her ex.

Being divorced from my miserable old life did reignite some feeling of being young, and I used to love to go dancing, so I showered, slipped into my favorite jeans, a sleeveless blouse and some heels. We drank a few beers before we headed out the door and to the Aquarius Club to dance the night away.

I noticed Sam immediately. He looked sexy in his blue jeans and black t-shirt, very different from his deli uniform of a white shirt and burgundy apron. He walked onto the dance floor to talk to one of his friends who was dancing with a cute young blond girl. He was so big and attractive; the beer was making me brave and making me forget that I was too old to be in that club. I grabbed Teresa and pulled her out to the middle of the dance floor, hoping to get Sam's attention and bumping into him to ensure that I did.

A few weeks ago, I'd been eating in the deli almost daily, leaving change in the tip jar, clearing my own table and smiling at him without so much as a smile in return. Now here he was, not at work, not in his uniform and not with a girl. I just wanted him to recognize me, acknowledge me.

He saw Teresa first. Then he saw me. He grabbed his friend away from the cute blond to dance with Teresa and turned to dance with me. *Finally*. He was smooth on the dance floor, his dancing was sexy but subtle. "I'm Amanda," I yelled to him over the music. "I've seen you at the deli where I sometimes eat lunch."

"Is that right?" he said with a surprised look.

"Yeah," I said, squinting at him, shocked and a little pissed that he didn't recognize me. "I work at the travel agency down the street." He either didn't hear me or ignored me and kept dancing. Clearly, he wasn't interested in me. *God, I'm so stupid. I gotta get out of here. I'm too old for this.* I danced until the song was over then turned around to leave the dance floor.

Sam grabbed my arm and said, "Let me get your number."

"Really?" I said, puzzled. "Okay." Walking toward the bar to get a napkin and a pen, I impulsively asked, "Do you have a girlfriend?"

"No. Do you have a boyfriend?"

"No," I laughed while writing down my phone number. After taking the napkin with my phone number, he hollered at a friend, turned and walked away; he didn't say thank you, nice meeting you, or I'll call you tomorrow; he just turned around and walked away from me, cutting through the crowd of people. I was confused and wanted to forget him, but the truth was that the less interested he was in me, the more interested I was in him.

I joined Teresa standing at a table talking to a couple of guys. I kept scanning the crowd for Sam and wondering if he would find me to say goodbye before he left or if I would hear from him again. Doubting either would happen, I decided I'd never eat at the deli again.

When Teresa and I called it a night, the two guys walked us out to the parking lot. The four of us were laughing and joking around when a big, old, brown car with a loud muffler pulled up. Sam rolled down the window and said, "I'm going to call you tomorrow."

I leaned in the window and smelled his scent of cologne, his leather jacket and cigarette smoke. It was intoxicating. I wanted to lean in and bury my face in his neck. I wanted to feel his skin against mine. "Sure you will." I smiled.

He didn't smile back, but he did turn his head to check out the two guys standing with Teresa. Then he smiled as if thinking there was a possibility I was going home with one of them. That smile made me lose interest in everybody but Sam.

Chapter 3

THAT WEEKEND, I didn't sit home by the phone. I went to the gym, and on the way home I picked up some groceries and my drycleaning. I was pretty sure Sam wouldn't call and though I was a little disappointed, a part of me was glad—Sam seemed like trouble.

On Monday morning while I was eating cheese from my lunch bag, Sam walked into Streamline Travel Agency wearing his deli uniform. "So this is where you work?" he asked.

"That's what I told you," I said, irritated.

He smiled, then laughed. "I like you. You're feisty."

Sara, my best friend and co-worker, rolled her eyes before answering the phone.

"I'm taking lunch early," I told her as I grabbed my jacket and purse from my desk drawer and followed Sam outside.

"You didn't call me like you said you were going to." Not answering, Sam pulled me to him, pressed me against the building and kissed me. "What are you doing?" I said, not letting my body react. Then I walked toward the alley to get out of site of the agency.

"What are you doing tonight? I want to come over."

"I don't know anything about you. Who are you?"

"I'll come over tonight and fill you in."

"Funny!"

"Not like that. Come here," he said, pulling me to him by my wrists. He held my face in his hands and kissed me. This time I let my body go. I couldn't believe I was kissing somebody other than Nick and I pressed my face against his warm neck breathing in that same intoxicating mixture of cologne, leather and cigarette smoke. I didn't know this man at all but his mysteriousness infatuated me. Sam seemed to have two settings—coming on strong or completely unavailable. I had never met anybody like him, and I couldn't wait to learn more about him. I gave him my address, and we set up a dinner date for later that night.

When Sam came over to pick me up for our date, Teresa let him in and led him back to my room. I wasn't ready; I was dressed but not sure about my outfit, my hair was still wet and I was sitting on my bed, which was just a mattress on the floor—I hadn't fought the divorce settlement because I'd just wanted out of the marriage and the fighting was getting too painful. Nick's demands of getting everything in hopes of getting me back, didn't work. Besides, I wanted Nick to find a nice young wife to give him children, and the couple of months of freedom had changed me and there was no going back. I wanted my life back. I wanted to find myself.

"Why aren't you ready?" Sam asked.

"I don't know," I said and opened my legs wide letting my red skirt slip up on my hips. I knew I was acting ridiculous, but I couldn't help myself. I hadn't had sex in almost two years. I wanted to flirt and tease and be young and sexy.

"I know what you're doing and it's not going to work," he said. "I told you I'd be here at seven to pick you up." He didn't smile. He didn't laugh. He didn't get aroused.

"I had to work late."

"You should have called me."

"I don't have your number."

He thought for a moment. "You're right." He sat down on the chair by my desk. "Well, hurry up."

I smiled.

He smiled back and said, "You look good with wet hair."

"Thanks." That was one compliment I'd never heard before. I grinned and opened my legs again to give him another quick look at my lime green panties before I stood up to go to the bathroom.

"I saw them the first time," he said. "Hurry up." He was not affected by me. He was cool and calm, yet authoritative and sexy. I liked him whether we were to become lovers or not.

After I dried my hair, I went back to the bedroom. Sam was still sitting at my desk with his arms folded in front of him. "Are you almost ready?" he asked impatiently.

The more irritated he was, the more irritating I became. It was like a game—who could frustrate the other more. I got down on my knees pushing my ass out searching for some shoes in my closet— three pairs of high heels. I slipped into two different shoes and asked, "Which do you like better, the black ones or the red ones?"

"Just pick something," he said, then pointed. "I like the red ones."

"Okay, do you like the red ones better than these other black ones?" I asked.

Sam stood up then walked to the bedroom doorway. "I'll wait in the car."

"Okay, okay," I laughed and grabbed his hand.

He leaned over and gave me a kiss. "Thanks for going out with me tonight."

"Thanks for inviting me." Smelling his intoxicating scent again, I asked, "Do you smoke?"

"A little."

Not expecting that answer, I was taken aback. When I first smelled the smoke on him, I'd assumed he had friends at the bar who smoked and the smell was still on him. *Should be a deal breaker, but if he only smokes a little, I can get him to quit.*

We said goodbye to Teresa and walked to his car—the same big, brown, ugly car that made him seem like trailer trash. "Let's take my car," I insisted. "I have to get gas before work tomorrow anyway. But you drive," I said, handing him the keys.

He had no problem taking the keys to my newer white Honda Accord, and as we drove to the restaurant, I was impressed by his driving, considering it was his first time driving my car. He was fast but careful, and could parallel park effortlessly. *Parallel park!* I couldn't, so it was a magical skill to me. And, of course, a little sexual innuendo crept into my mind about how his ability to parallel park must reflect his ability to perform sexually.

I was already sure I wanted to have sex with him, but I wasn't sure when I wanted it to happen. I knew the right thing to do was to wait and get to know him, but I didn't want to wait. I knew he wasn't right for me so maybe this would be that fling to rebound me back into the game of love. His lack of interest in me was making me crazy.

At dinner, he was his usual aloof self, so I did most of the talking. "I'm forty. I was married for fourteen years. Not sure what I want anymore. I thought I knew when I got married. I thought I would have a couple of kids and live happily ever after, but I guess it just wasn't meant to be. Being single is new to me again, so I'm just taking it one day at a time and trying to build a new life for myself. I'm at the travel agency for now but sometimes I think I would like to finish school, get my degree and become a counselor," I said, not convinced it was true.

"You? A counselor?" He laughed sarcastically.

"Yes," I laughed, too. "I'd be a good counselor. I care about people and I want to see everybody happy. Isn't that what we all strive for, happiness?"

"Sure."

"Are you happy?"

"Some days."

"Do you like working at the deli?"

"No."

"What are your goals? Did you go to school?"

"Yes, I went to school. I had a scholarship to play basketball." He seemed uncomfortable.

"What did you study?"

"I only made it the first semester," he said, then looked down and around as if looking for a way to change the subject.

I decided to back off of the personal questions. "Want to split a dessert?"

After dinner, we held hands and walked on the path down by the river, something I would never do alone at night but with Sam I felt safe. We didn't talk much, but he did kiss me every time we stopped to gaze at the dark river.

"Tell me about your family. Do you have sisters?"

"Eight."

I started laughing, "You do not!"

"Yes, and two brothers."

"Wow! What was that like growing up?"

"I'm the youngest by about ten years."

"Were you an accident?"

"I guess you could say that. Probably spoiled, too."

"Well, of course, the baby is always spoiled. I'm the baby of two older brothers. I'm doubly spoiled because I'm the only girl."

"And what was that like growing up?"

"A blast! Big brothers rock!" I smiled up at him.

"Where is your family? Here in town?" he asked.

I sat down on a bench. "No, they live up north. My parents and one brother, Teddy, who's a chef, live in Duluth. My oldest brother,

Rob, the normal one, lives in Minneapolis with his wife and kids. He's a lawyer."

"How'd you end up in Rochester?"

"I thought I wanted to be a nurse, so I moved here when I was twenty-four. But then one night, my friend, Sara, was drunk and we were at a party, jumping on a trampoline, and she broke her ankle."

Sam sat down next to me.

"I've always told people that I realized I didn't like needles or blood, and I don't, but the truth is, I can't stand to see people hurt. When I see somebody in physical pain, I physically get sick. I feel like I'm going to pass out or throw up." I turned toward him and smiled. "I'm sure you can imagine how that night turned out with Sara—she had to comfort me. I had to keep leaving the emergency room to get some fresh air or throw cold water on my face. I couldn't get a grip. When the doctor was moving Sara's foot, I could see the pain on her face and I almost blacked out. I had to get out of there. I left my friend in the hospital alone. That's when I knew I couldn't be a nurse." I hadn't told many people the truth because I hated looking and feeling so vulnerable and weak. "So, I thought counseling—I could still help people but their pain wouldn't be so obvious."

"When are you going to finish school?"

"I don't know. After I got married, my husband convinced me to quit school because he thought I was under too much stress. We were trying to have a baby, which we'd been trying to do our entire marriage. I think that was one of the main reasons we fell apart, I can't have kids. He resented me, and I became a miserable person."

Sam pulled me to him and held me as if letting me know it was okay to cry. But I didn't cry. I had cried most of my marriage and I just didn't have another tear to shed over my failed marriage or my inability to have kids. I was okay and ready to move forward with different dreams.

I slowly pulled away from Sam. "Thank you," I said, and then returned to the subject of school. "I didn't go to school right after high school either. I had plans to travel. I wanted to find my calling."

"Is counseling your calling?"

"I doubt it. Maybe that's why I haven't returned. I don't know what I want. I never seem to know what I want."

Sam stood up and said, "Let's head back." He pulled me up, and we slowly walked back to my car in silence.

At home, Sam walked me to my door and handed over my car keys. After we kissed goodnight, I watched him walk to his car. With his strong, protective character, I felt small and childlike around him, I imagined that he had done a lot of living in his years.

I wondered if we would have another date.

Chapter 4

I DIDN'T SEE or hear from Sam for several days after our first date. Disappointed, I figured I had talked too much, but then felt defensive because somebody had to. I assumed he wasn't interested, but I was drawn to him and my heart was already feeling the loss. Sam was exciting, and my life was sorely lacking excitement.

Friday on my lunch break, I couldn't resist walking slowly by the deli in hopes of running into him. I glanced in the windows but only saw my own reflection—I noticed that I was still slouching my shoulders, so I quickly straightened up. *Grow up! So my first date after divorce wasn't great, big deal.* I told myself he wasn't a good fit anyway: he smoked, he worked at a deli with seemingly no goals and he was probably really poor from the looks of his beat-up, old car. I wanted more from a partner. I wanted more for me.

That night, I was in my pajamas planning to finish reading my romance novel with only fifty or so pages to go. Teresa was on a fourth date with her new boyfriend, and we were both pretty sure she would be spending the night at his place. Around nine o'clock, there was a knock at the door. Not saying anything, Sam stepped swiftly into the apartment and pulled me to him. His body was so masculine and vigorous, and I felt helpless in his arms. He kissed me hard and led me into the bedroom. He lay on top of me kissing me, caressing me. No words were spoken. We wanted each other and we gave in.

When we finished, I couldn't stop smiling. It felt amazing to be with a man again. He lay on his side, facing me, and said, "You're my girlfriend."

"I don't think so. We had a nice night and then you don't call me for days… my boyfriend would never do that to me."

"You're my girlfriend now," he said and smiled.

"We'll see."

He wasn't right for me. He wasn't what I envisioned in a partner. He wasn't somebody I'd want to show off to family and friends. But he fulfilled something inside me that was longing for him, longing for a man just like him. I was intoxicated by every scent, every touch, every word he spoke and every moment I was with him. How could I ever get enough of him? I was afraid of loving him from the start. He was like fire and I knew I'd get burned but I couldn't stop letting his flame engulf me. Sam rolled back on top of me and entered me again.

I woke up with Sam sleeping next to me. I watched him. I studied him. I knew why I was with him, I had read enough self-help books—that's all I read during my marriage—but I wanted a little drama and some good crazy sex. And maybe I needed a little self-punishment for staying in my marriage so long. This would pass. This fling would end and I would return to my normal life. But I was going to enjoy him while I had him.

Sam opened his eyes and turned his head in my direction. "Good morning."

I smiled. "Good morning."

He pulled me close to him and we made love again.

After he made us scrambled eggs with cheese and buttered toast, we decided to take a shower together. He wanted to go again while in the shower, but I was sore and said no.

"Okay, give me head then."

"That's funny," I said sarcastically.

"Come on, it's your duty. You're my girlfriend."

"You are really something! And I'm not your girlfriend."

Sam reached for me and I stepped up onto the shower bench so we were closer to the same height. He held me close to him, swaying as if we were slow dancing in the shower. He kissed me several times but made no more attempts to make love. "I'm crazy about you, Amanda." He wrapped his big arms around me and my heart leapt in dread and delight. I wanted him to be crazy about me, but my heart already hurt, fearing this wasn't right and somebody would get hurt.

Sam left before Teresa got home and I didn't tell her. Instead, I listened to her tell me every detail about her date and the sex and their life plans—but in my mind, nothing could compare to the night I'd just had. I pretended to be interested, and any other time I would have been, but this morning all I could do was think about Sam, his black hair, his strong facial features, every sound he made while he slept, every word he spoke to me, every time he made me laugh. My night with Sam was more engrossing than anything Teresa could have told me about her night. I wanted to relive and savor every detail of my wonderful romance.

I did want to tell Teresa about Sam, but I knew so little. I didn't know where he lived, I didn't have his phone number, and I didn't even know his last name. And I didn't know when I'd see him again. Maybe keeping him a secret was best. Maybe I was a fool and I was being used. Maybe my secret was Sam's secret, too. But this didn't stop me from longing to be in his arms again.

Chapter 5

MONDAY AT WORK, I had an unwelcome visit from my ex-husband. Nick liked to harass me from time to time, usually at work where I'd feel most vulnerable and embarrassed. But luckily this time, I was the only one in the office.

"Can't you just leave me alone?" I said, and took a deep breath. "Nick, you have to move on. I can't give you kids and you want kids. I wasn't happy, and you weren't happy. We don't like the same things. We drifted apart and neither of us tried to fix it."

"We can adopt," he said.

"It's not what I want anymore. You can't keep stopping by my office. You're going to make me lose my job. It's been months, you kicked *me* out, remember? It's time for you to get over it."

"I just want to talk. I made some mistakes, but so did you."

"We've talked, Nick. Four months ago, remember? I was on my knees at my old front door, begging you to take me back. Do you have any idea how humiliating that was to have you close the door in my face, just after telling me how miserable I was and laughing at me?"

"You're such a bitch!" he snapped.

"Wow, Nick. Thanks for making this so easy. You have to go."

"I'm not leaving until you agree to talk to me."

"Ugh." I put my head down on the desk and I heard the door open. I looked up and saw Sam in the doorway. He said nothing to me and didn't even look at me. He looked at Nick and said, "Hey, man. Can I talk to you for a second out here?"

Nick walked outside with Sam, completely unaware that I knew this giant of a man. With Sam towering over him, they exchanged a few words and Nick left. Sam opened the door and peeked inside. "You okay?"

"Yeah, fine."

"I don't think he'll bother you anymore."

I was stunned. "Thanks."

"I'll see you later," he said and left.

I didn't know what to think about what had happened, but I did expect another harassing phone call or another visit from Nick. But several days later when I saw Nick at Target, he ignored me. He looked right at me and looked away with his head down. I suddenly felt sadness. I didn't want to see Nick hurting, but I also felt a sense of power having Sam on my side.

I wondered how Sam knew that Nick was bothering me. *How did he know? Did I have a look on my face? Or did he hear the conversation?* It was odd and I had mixed feelings but for the most part, Sam wanting to protect me, felt comforting.

Sam and I started spending more time together, sometimes at his place and sometimes at mine, usually when Teresa was staying with her boyfriend, Jim. But after only a couple of months, problems in our relationship became more and more evident. We were past the rebound or fling stage, but I still didn't know about our future. We were not affectionate in public. We didn't touch, kiss or hold hands. I hadn't met any of his friends or family, and he had only met Teresa and Sara on my side. I wasn't sure if subconsciously he was my secret lover or if I was his.

I came up with the bright idea to drive to Minneapolis with Sam so he could meet my brother and his family. I thought this would be a good test to see if we had potential or if our relationship was purely sexual. Rob and his wife, Kelly, were wonderful people, and they were anxious for me to find a better man than Nick. I think they still secretly blamed Nick for our failure to have children. Kelly was convinced that with the right man I could have a baby and give her children a cousin. They pressured Teddy, too, but I knew my brother was pretty content not having the responsibility of children yet.

Surprisingly, Sam agreed to go, but on the drive to Rob's place, he argued and picked fights with me the entire hour and a half. He went so far as to say he didn't want to meet my family because he wasn't wearing good socks. When we reached the intersection to turn left to go to Rob's, I'd had enough. "If you don't want to meet my brother, just say so! I can't take this!"

"I don't want to meet your brother."

"Why?"

"I don't know, I don't know," he said, looking bewildered and hurt.

"Fine!" I said coldly and headed back toward Rochester. I called Rob on my cellphone and told him that I wasn't feeling well and we'd have to take a raincheck. Hardly speaking on the drive back, we both knew that this was a critical moment in our short relationship. I wanted to cry, even though deep down I was glad he hadn't met Rob and his family. I didn't want them to meet a man I was having doubts about myself, somebody who probably would never fit into my life, or theirs, in any long term sort of way.

It started raining, a fitting end to a dreary day. Sam reached into the glove compartment and pulled out the Al Green CD he had bought for me. He slipped it into the CD player, and put his hand on my leg as I drove. I feared our unusual relationship was coming to an end. I wasn't sure if I or Sam would end it, but I knew it would hurt either way.

Chapter 6

WHEN WE GOT to my place, we went straight to my bedroom and closed the door. He sat in the chair with his elbows resting on his knees and his head hanging. "I'm sorry. I guess I just wasn't ready to meet your family."

My heart ached. I didn't know if I wanted him forever, but I so desperately wanted the right man to want me forever, and Sam wasn't that man.

"I love you, Amanda."

"What do you mean?" I cried. "We haven't met each other's friends and we're not going to either, are we? You don't love me. You don't even hold hands with me at the mall," I said, wiping my eyes."

He sat down next to me on the mattress and kissed me. "Yes, we are," he said, as he gently brushed the hair from my face. His eyes were sad. "I'm sorry I let you down."

"It's not that you let me down. I think this thing we have is ending and I'm sad."

Sam put his head down again and whispered, "It's not ending, at least not from me."

I wanted to break up with him, for it to be over, and to blame him for the problems. But I had never reached for Sam's hand either and having him meet my brother had been a test that we'd both failed. Searching for the words, I heard myself say, "I don't want to break up."

Sam pushed me back onto the bed. With one hand, he managed to open my blouse and remove my jeans as he eased himself inside me, both of us passionately desperate to keep our relationship alive and deepen our connection.

The next morning after getting breakfast at McDonald's, Sam and I sat in his big brown car parked by Silver Lake. I stared at the cigarette butts in the ashtray and the ashes on the floor while he lectured me.

He asked me why I was acting so crazy, something my husband used to say to me, especially while I was on hormonal therapy. "You better figure out why you're holding me at a distance. And you better decide what you want before this goes any further," he said. "I'm not playing these games with you."

"I think *you're* acting crazy!" I snapped back.

"Oh do you?" he said and gently nudged my shoulder.

"I'm serious. I'm not kidding." I said, trying to keep a straight face as he sat grinning at me. "What do *you* want?"

Sam became serious and he said with great conviction, "I want to love you forever."

My heart was suddenly in my throat. I loved having him around and I loved the sex but I was making terrible decisions and I didn't know how to stop myself. I wasn't ready to walk away. I wasn't ready to be alone again.

After analyzing and dissecting our relationship issues, we agreed to stop pressuring each other and to continue seeing each other. And then he shocked me with an invitation to join him on a long-weekend road trip to Chicago in a couple of weeks. He was going to visit his family and some friends, and he wanted me with him. I'd never been to Chicago but always wanted to go. Around the same time I begged Nick to take me back, my work had sent most of the office to Chicago for training. I was the one who had to stay behind and I was devastated. But now I had the chance to see Chicago and I couldn't wait. We could do some sightseeing and get to know each other better—and I could meet some of his friends.

Maybe this will be the key to getting our relationship on the right track.

Chapter 7

WE TOOK TIME off work and planned for our quick trip to Illinois. July was a slow month for me at the agency anyway because nobody really wanted to travel away from Minnesota in the beautiful summer weather. We left right after work on Thursday, with all my favorite CDs picked out for the trip and Sam with just his one Al Green CD. We had snacks, pop and bottles of water for the six-hour drive to the windy city.

Sam opened up a lot in the intimacy of the car. He told me how his mom used to listen to Al Green all the time and that was comfort music for him. He talked about his sisters and brothers, and a little about his family with too many people to name. He had nephews who were older than him, which took me a few seconds to figure out that some of his sisters were old enough to be his mother. And he finally told me he was thirty-three years old.

When there was a lull in the conversation, I popped in one of my dance CDs. I was on a road trip to someplace I'd never been. I was traveling, doing what I've always wanted to do. I felt free and crazy and overjoyed to be getting out of Rochester and away from my roommate and co-workers. I felt closer to Sam than ever, and got aroused watching him drive down the dark highway. I pulled off my jeans and panties, leaned over and started unzipping his pants. To my surprise, he let me and he was already hard. I knew he expected me to give him head but I had a better idea. I faced him, straddled him and forced him deep inside me.

He kept driving, slowing down just a little. Then he became nervous when a car behind started to rapidly gain on us. When the car passed us, he sighed in relief and we continued our over the road sex session. When we finished, we were both surprised by what we had just done. We laughed while playing out the different scenarios: What if that had been a cop? What if we got in an accident? I trusted Sam because he always seemed calmly in control of the situation, whether it was having sex while driving down the road, working at the deli or making sure I was protected.

Late that night we rolled into his stomping ground, and it became clear to me that he hadn't warned me about any aspect of his life. Finding what looked like the nicest motel in the area, we walked over to the Plexiglas window to get a room and the big woman asked, "Four hours or eight?"

Not understanding, I turned and looked at Sam.

He stepped up to the window and said, "Eight."

Then I got it and I wasn't thrilled about staying there. *That window is not Plexiglas; it's bullet proof.* Realizing this part of the city was dangerous, I said, "Sam, I don't want to stay here!"

Ignoring me, he got the room key, and said, "Come on."

I followed him as he carried our bags up the stairs to our room. I tried to slam the door but it was broken. "This door doesn't shut tight. Oh my God, I don't think this is safe. Sam, I have a credit card, let's go stay someplace nice."

He lifted the door slightly and closed it so that it latched. He turned the deadbolt, then asked me to give him any cash, credit cards or valuables I had. After I handed him my wallet, he lifted the mattress slightly and put his wad of cash and my wallet beneath it. After glancing out the window, he pulled a broken chair from beside the table and nudged it under the doorknob. "This is where I grew up," he said and went into the bathroom.

A little shocked and very tired, I hadn't expected this. But I wasn't going to argue, I just wanted to go to sleep. It was so late, I figured we should get a wake-up call to be sure we were out of there in the eight hours we paid for. I picked up the phone, which was lying on the floor, and dialed the front desk. The woman seemed to be talking to somebody else and hung up on me.

Sam stepped out of the bathroom and stared at me while I held the phone. I turned and dialed the front desk again. "Yes, this is room 210. Could we get a wake-up call at…" She hung up on me again.

"Ugh," I said, looking at Sam, and he was shaking his head as if I were foolish. "What? Do you have an alarm clock?" I asked.

He shook his head again and sighed as he walked past me to adjust the curtains. "Let's go to bed."

Trying to be lighthearted, I joked, "Now that's not very romantic." I dug into my suitcase, pulled out my sexy little nightgown, and I walked into the bathroom. It was disgusting. I put a towel on the floor to step on before changing clothes. I didn't sit on the toilet while going to the bathroom, and decided to skip washing my face or brushing my teeth.

Sam was still standing by the window when I stepped out of the bathroom. "You okay?" I asked.

"Yeah." He turned and said, "Sorry about this place."

"No, it's nice. I like it," I said and grinned. I knew he wasn't buying it.

He wrapped his arms around me and I wrapped my legs around his waist. We made love in the four-hour or eight-hour motel room somewhere deep in the seedy side of Chicago.

Chapter 8

WHEN I AWOKE the next morning, Sam was already up and again looking out the window. Lifting the sheet in the slight morning light, I realized the sheets were not clean. I slipped out of bed and prayed I hadn't caught anything. The morning wasn't looking great and I wanted a Starbucks coffee, a venti double-raspberry mocha, to try to find some normalcy, some comfort.

Still groggy, I walked into the bathroom and it looked worse than it had the night before. It was old and filthy, the toilet didn't stop running and the faucet had a broken handle. I peeked behind the nasty shower curtain and saw more disgusting filth; the white tub was grossly discolored with lots of black hair still in it. *How did I get here?* I stepped back out and said, smiling, "That bathroom's a mess."

"Let's shower and get out of here," Sam answered and reached into his duffel bag. "Do you want to go first?"

"Ah, no, you go ahead." I wanted him to at least rinse it out with his own germs.

"I'll be quick," he said and looked at me. "Don't open that door. Don't leave this room."

"Oh, I was going to go get us some coffee at Starbucks," I said sarcastically and grinned.

Not smiling, he stepped behind the bathroom door.

Sam made me laugh. He got my sense of humor and sarcasm, but he always acted mad and that tickled me. He knew that opening that door was the last thing I wanted to do. I would never be in a situation like this with any other man, but with Sam for some reason, it was okay.

I pulled out some clothes from the suitcase, but couldn't decide where to lay them, so I set them back on my suitcase. I took out my makeup bag and put on my cross necklace. Out of curiosity, I stepped over to my side of the bed, kneeled on the filthy carpet and lifted the mattress slightly. I wondered if others stashed their valuables under the mattress and maybe forgot to collect them. Seeing something, I lifted the mattress further and cried out, "Oh my God!" There was a bent spoon, some cotton and a syringe.

"Don't touch it!" Sam yelled at me just as I was about to touch it.

"I'm not!" I snapped and pulled my hand back.

"Yes, you were going to! Put the mattress down." He stepped toward me. "Jesus, Amanda! Don't touch shit like that!"

"Okay! I heard you! I've just never seen anything like that before."

"Get in the shower. We gotta get out of here."

The last thing Sam did before we left the room was get our stuff out from under his side of the mattress. Our first stop was the apartment of two of his sisters, who were even older than I expected. They were very poor and hadn't taken good care of themselves, leading me to assume they were both on welfare or disability. But their generosity and kindness made me crazy about them and to see the love they had for Sam was very touching.

We visited over eggs and toast, the best eggs I'd ever had, or maybe I was just starving. His sisters had a good laugh when they saw how small I was next to Sam. "The way Sammy talks about you, I expected you to be seven-foot tall, almighty powerful one. But you're so little, not at all what we expected."

I was flattered and surprised that Sam had mentioned me, even more pleased that he had spoken about me as if I were important to him. I hadn't really told my family about him. His whole life was a mystery to me, so I was happy to learn that he was capable of communication. After a few hours, we reluctantly said our goodbyes because we had a lot of people to see. They both gave me a warm, accepting hug before Sam and I left their apartment.

Our next stop was a visit to one of his best friends, Adrian, who lived in an even worse area—graffiti everywhere, boarded-up buildings and houses, people just hanging out, doing nothing. I followed Sam up the cluttered stairway of a house that had been turned into apartments. At a door on the second floor, Sam knocked. A TV blared from another apartment and there was rustling behind the door Sam knocked on. "What!"

"Open the fuck'n door, man!"

The door flew open and there stood a thin, tall man. "Wuzzup?" A huge smile covered his face, they hugged, and he said, "Come in, come in." When he turned to lead the way to the living room, I could see a silver pistol tucked into the back of his pants. "Sit, sit," Adrian said to me.

I cautiously sat on one end of his afghan-covered couch while Sam sat down on the quilt-covered chair and Adrian on the other end of the couch.

"So wuzzup? What're you doing here? Visiting your sistas?"

"Yeah."

"Aw, we all miss you around here, man. You gonna see your mamma, too?

"Yeah."

"Man, it's so great you got outta here. It's gett'n crazier every day. Proud of you, man, proud of you." He stood up and gave Sam another quick hug. "But you gotta get back more often."

I felt like a fly on the wall. There had been no introduction and no acknowledgement that I was even in the room. Sam's strange lack of manners intrigued me and I was beginning to see Sam more clearly, as I learned bits and pieces about him.

Adrian pulled his gun out and set it on the coffee table. He leaned back to get more comfortable on the couch. I did, too, kicking off my shoes and crossing my legs in front of me.

Pointing at me with his thumb and looking at Sam, Adrian said, "What's this?"

"Nothing but trouble, trust me," Sam said and smiled.

"All right, all right, I gotcha." Adrian gave me the once over, laughed and gave Sam a quick fist bump. "It's Friday night, so what's going on tonight?"

"She wants to go dancing."

"What! Dancing?" he yelled and turned to me. "Go get yo'self a muthafuck'n record player and dance in your room!"

Sam burst out laughing.

"You don't need to be out there," Adrian cautioned.

I didn't get what he was trying to say until later—too dangerous for a woman like me to go dancing at the Click or anyplace in that part of Chicago. Or maybe he thought I was too old. Either way, I needed some exercise and dancing seemed like the best way to get it.

After our forty-five minute visit, Adrian grabbed his gun and walked us down to the car. He gave me a huge hug before we left and told me to bring Sam back to Chicago more often.

Our next stop was *oh, so secretive* and only a few blocks from Adrian's place, with the same depressing surroundings—boarded-up houses, graffiti-covered buildings and idle people, even children. Sam told me to lock the doors and wait in the car, and he went into a house with houses boarded up on each side. A few minutes later, he came out with a tall woman and a young girl. The girl got into the backseat, and the woman walked around to my side of the car and said, "Hi, nice to meet you, Amanda."

I looked at Sam for an explanation.

"Amanda, this is my daughter, Danielle. And this is her mother, Danae."

I almost choked, trying to hide my shock, I said, "Hi, Danielle. It's so nice to meet you."

Danae started laughing then snapped at Sam, "You didn't tell her?" She bent over leaning in the window. "Yes, I know, he's a man of few words," she said and giggled.

"We're taking Danielle shopping and out to dinner," Sam said to me, then turned to Danae, saying, "We should have her home by eight."

"Okay, have fun, honey," Danae said to Danielle and waved.

I tried to get a grip on my feelings but I was angry and hurt. He knew I couldn't have kids; I told him on our first date. And he didn't care enough about me or my feelings to tell me he has a child. *Of all the opportunities he's had to tell me, he decides to spring it on me like this.* I closed my eyes and shook my head in disbelief that Sam had a daughter. With my mind blurry with anger I listened as Sam and Danielle made small talk. I wanted to cry, but this wasn't Danielle's fault so I pulled myself together, turned around in my seat and started talking to Danielle. "So, how old are you?

"Eight."

"And your favorite color is?"

"Purple."

"Oh, good color."

"What's your favorite color?" she asked me.

"I like purple, too," I said. "What's your favorite number?"

"Three."

"Ah, mine too! Don't tell me your favorite meal is spaghetti?"

"I love spaghetti!"

"But is it your favorite? Because it's my favorite."

"Yes, it's my favorite," she said and giggled.

I turned to Sam. "Can you believe this?"

"No, I can't," he said and squeezed my leg.

We pulled into the parking lot of Payless Shoes and got out of the car. Danielle raced over to me and grabbed my hand. My heart dropped, and I was in love with her—madly, crazy in love with this girl. She was the little girl I always wanted. I had a lump in my throat and I held back the tears. I wanted to save her from where she was growing up. I wanted to give her everything I had. I looked at Sam and nodded my head—I was getting in way too deep. I held on tightly to Danielle's hand, and wondered if I could hold on tightly to Sam and every piece of baggage that came with him if it meant that Danielle could be a part of my life.

Danielle was the cutest, sweetest little girl I had ever been around. She was thoughtful and polite, with the manners of a girl growing up in the finest families. Sam and Danae were doing the best job they could raising her, considering the environment in which she lived.

We held hands and walked through the deserted store to the row of size six shoes, only one size smaller than my own. She said she needed tennis shoes, so we found that section. I found a pair that were white with purple in her size so she tried them on and walked around. She said she loved them and they were the ones she wanted. We headed to the front of the store where we found Sam by the cash register. Another man, who looked a little rough, had come into the store. When Danielle and I walked by him, he quietly made a "Mmm-mmm" sound. It made me uncomfortable, but I ignored it and hoped Danielle didn't hear him. At the counter, I pulled out my wallet to buy the shoes for Danielle; it was going to be my treat.

After the three of us were in the car, Sam said, "Wait here, I'll be right back." He left the car running and went back into the store. Through the windows, I could see him approaching the rundown man inside. I saw Sam hover over this man as he had done with Nick. His size was intimidating enough but when he leaned over someone, I couldn't imagine that person crossing him.

Trying to figure out why he went back into the store and what problem he had with that man, I asked Sam, "What was that about?"

"I potentially just saved his life."

"What do you mean?"

"He can't look at you like that and be so disrespectful toward you, my daughter and me. I just gave him a little lesson," he said and put the car in reverse.

I wasn't sure if I was tired or crabby, but I was starting to see more parts of Sam I didn't like than parts I did.

Danielle was admiring her new shoes, seemingly ignoring the conversation, but I was pretty sure she knew what had just happened and what her dad was talking about. I changed the subject and looked in the backseat. "Where can we get some good spaghetti, or whatever Danielle wants?"

Sam drove to a better area and we found a nice little Italian restaurant. I loved watching Sam interact with his daughter; he was strict, but loving. I began to understand why Sam drove an old brown car and worked at the deli. The deli, owned by a bigger company, was union, so he had insurance and Danielle was on his insurance. I understood his first priority would always be his daughter and I respected and admired him for taking that responsibility.

After one of the best dinners I'd ever had, we found a great discount clothing store and I bought Danielle several new outfits. I wanted to help Sam and Danielle so I paid for everything. I paid for the shoes at Payless, dinner at the Italian restaurant and all of

Danielle's new clothes. Maybe it was guilt, because I was feeling the need to pull away from Sam.

Chapter 9

AFTER WE DROPPED off Danielle, I insisted we stay in a better hotel in a better area. He agreed and I put the Holiday Inn charge on my credit card. I was glad to stay in a clean, safe room, with a nightly rate, not an hourly rate, and wake-up calls.

"So tonight we're going dancing," he said as he reached for his pack of cigarettes and headed for the door. "I'm going to call some friends."

I jumped in the clean shower with my shampoo, conditioner and toothbrush and toothpaste—I loved to brush my teeth in the shower. I took my time getting ready, noticing that Sam looked out of place and had seemed more at home at the seedy motel. It made me sad that he had such a hard life. He grew up in the toughest, poorest Chicago neighborhoods.

We drove back into some rougher areas to pick up his friends, who I later learned were his cousins. I offered to get in the back seat because his friends were almost as big as Sam and I thought it made more sense because I was so much smaller.

"No, stay where you are," Sam said. The guys climbed in back, grunting while they fit themselves into the tight space.

"You guys, here, somebody get in front..."

"Guys, get out. I gotta talk to her," Sam said, cutting me off.

His cousins gladly got back out of the car and stood by the trunk talking. Sam leaned over. "You are with me. You will always sit next to me. Don't ever crawl your ass in the back seat of a car. You are too good for that. Do you hear what I'm saying? This is your car. You sit beside me; you're not less important than me or them. They can sit in the back. That's where they should sit. Do you understand?"

"Yes, I understand," I said, feeling like I was being disciplined for trying to be considerate. His lectures were making me feel like his eight-year-old daughter. I'd had my moments of believing Sam was misunderstood and with enough love and patience he'd come around. But now, I feared that Sam was controlling and that kind of scared me. Even if Sam was trying to tell me I was important to him, it felt more like he was telling me where I should sit, how I should feel, and what he expected of me—was this parallel to my relationship with Nick?

It was starting to make sense, if I continued this relationship, I would continue losing myself the same way I lost myself with Nick. I wasn't going to let it ruin the night. I'd made my bed. I took my risk with a guy like Sam, so I was going to ride it out. *I'll end it when we get back to Rochester.*

I was eager to burn off some of my frustration at the huge dance club that spilled pounding music into the streets. I had never before been in a club where I had to go through a metal detector, be patted down, and have my purse checked, but once we were inside we rushed to the dance floor and danced for a couple of hours. I danced with Sam's cousins and some of his friends. Sam continued running into people he knew and I was taken aback by how popular he really was. People genuinely seemed to like him. And after a night of fun and a couple of drinks, I kind of liked him again, too.

When I had to go to the bathroom, he walked me there and waited until I was finished. Once I was in the bathroom without my protective man by my side, I suddenly felt very alone and uneasy. All eyes were on me and the experience was new to me. The women were hanging out, sitting around, fixing their hair, fixing their friend's hair. It was crowded and I was clearly an outsider. Quickly doing my business, I left without washing my hands or checking my face.

When Sam and I were ready to go, his cousins told him they'd catch a ride with somebody else. We walked to my car and he leaned over and gave me a long, passionate kiss. "I love ya," he said.

I didn't say anything back because I didn't know how I felt. I didn't know how I would fit into his life or how he would fit into mine. I didn't know if I wanted to change my future plans to make room for him and Danielle and his Chicago life.

We passed a White Castle surrounded by police cars with their red and blue flashing lights. One of the large front windows was shattered. The police officers were standing around interviewing White Castle's customers. "Probably a drive by," Sam said. I shook my head in disbelief. This was quite an experience and one I wasn't taking lightly.

As we drove through the city streets of this different world, I became anxious to travel to new places. I felt lucky to have experienced Sam's background. He had helped open my eyes to another way of life, a different culture right here in the United States. *I want to experience life, I want to see new things and learn. I have nothing to tie me down.* I relaxed as we passed each streetlight and rundown building on our way back to the suburbs and our safe hotel.

Chapter 10

THE LAST COUPLE days of our Chicago trip were intense, as we spent time with Sam's mother, brothers and other sisters. Then the final day was spent with Danielle, who gave me a stuffed white dog to thank me for our visit. I had such mixed feelings. Truthfully, I was in love with his family, in love with his daughter, but I was not in love with Sam. Was there even enough of a connection to try to move forward?

Maybe I had learned too much about Sam all at once. Though he didn't communicate well, he took the chance of letting me into his life to meet his family and friends. Now it was up to me to decide if this was what I wanted. Sam's life seemed far too complicated. Sam was complicated. Sam and I were completely different from two completely different worlds.

I was looking forward to our drive back to Minnesota early Monday morning and being alone again, just the two of us for several hours. But our drive back was quiet, and Sam seemed distant. Maybe he was having his own doubts about me fitting into his life. Or maybe we were both just tired from the emotionally exhausting trip.

About thirty minutes from home, Sam started talking. "Well, you see what my life is all about. Do you want to be in my life?"

Shocked, I said, "Sam, that's great. Your life? I have a life too." I turned to him. "It's a lot to take in. You have a daughter that you never cared to mention."

"You can't have kids, so…"

"Are you serious? Are you serious? You have no clue how hurtful that is," I said and shook my head in disbelief. "And that's just it, you show me your life all at once and expect me to want to jump in, but you have never tried to find out about my life or what I want." I felt like I was dealing with Nick all over again. *What are you asking of me? What do you want?*

When we arrived at my apartment, he didn't come in with me. "Stop wasting my time, Amanda," Sam said. "Call me when you figure out what you want." And he left.

Sam had made a terrible mistake because I didn't cave in to ultimatums. That night, back in my apartment, I was happy to have my old life back, my pre-Sam life. It was Monday night and I had all day Tuesday to rest and relax away from Sam.

Teresa was home and fighting with her boyfriend, too. So we drank wine and talked about the men in our lives while I did laundry. "I just don't understand all the pushing and the pressure. And don't you think you tell somebody you've been seeing for a couple of months that you have a daughter? He's like a giant puzzle that he wants me to put together, take the time to make the pieces fit but with no help from him. And just like Nick, he's not interested in me or my wants. Not one bit."

"Did you tell him all of this?" Teresa asked.

I thought back to our conversation during the ride home. "Not in so many words."

"You might have to tell him; guys need things spelled out." she said and tilted her head to the side. "Even if you're just looking for understanding or closure."

"Closure," I repeated while sorting my whites from my dark clothes. I came across the panties I had worn on the way to Chicago when I seduced Sam while driving down the highway. "Maybe closure is a good idea. I don't know. I just can't figure this out."

"Do you ever think you're just as much of a puzzle to him? I mean, you came on strong and now you're backing way off."

"He has to change, I want to change him. I have a mental list of the things that need to change."

"You can't change him."

"I know, and that's the point, maybe I don't want a relationship. I mean, Jesus, Teresa, I haven't been divorced a year."

"But you're forty. Amanda, you're not honest with Sam or yourself. I can see right through you. Sam is not the one," she said, gently. "You know he's not the one!"

"Well, I guess not, I'm pretty sure it's over."

"Stop the games, Amanda. You need to end it."

I closed the lid on the washer. "Enough about me. What's going on with you two?" I asked, wanting to change the subject.

"Oh, it's nothing. He wants me to give him head, but he won't reciprocate."

I burst out laughing. "That's it?"

"Yep, that's it," she said and jumped off the dryer.

"You stand your ground!" I held up my glass.

She tapped her glass against mine, saying, "You too!"

"Let's go to Bakers Square for some pie!"

The next day, I cleaned the apartment, finished the laundry and went to the gym. I felt refreshed and ready for work the next morning. By six-thirty, it was clear that Sam wasn't going to call me. I painted my fingernails and toenails while watching a recorded episode of Oprah. Around nine, I headed to bed but couldn't stop thinking about Sam. I had spent almost every day with him for the last few months and now I was alone. I felt empty. The idea of us really being over made me forget about every reason he was wrong for me. *Why am I so afraid to be alone?* I secretly hoped he'd call. I just needed to give him space. *He'll call. He'll call,* I told myself as I drifted off to sleep.

Chapter 11

AFTER THREE WEEKS without Sam, I was a mess. Teresa even set me up with one of Jim's friends to help me get Sam out of my mind—somebody who resembled Brad Pit, somebody who would be impossible to resist. All my friends were hoping I would at least have sex with him to help speed up the process of getting over Sam. But when we ended up at my place and he tried to kiss me, I told him he had to go. I locked the door behind him and started to cry. I never dreamed at forty, I'd be divorced, childless, living in an apartment with a roommate, dating different men, going to bars. *Ugh! I'm such a mess.*

For the first time, I hated having the place to myself. Teresa had been spending almost every night with Jim. She was probably giving him head without requiring head in return, just for a place to stay so she wouldn't have to listen to me cry about all my problems. *I need to grow up!*

I considered calling Sam, but what would I say? What if Sam no longer wanted me? What if he did? I just couldn't believe it. I just couldn't believe that three weeks had passed with no phone call, no lunch date, no stopping by work to say hello. Work was torture knowing that every day I was less than a block away from him.

I survived my forty-first birthday with my parents and brothers but everybody was sick of me moping around. Even I was sick of me. So after one month of no contact with Sam, when Sara, my best friend from work, invited me to a party at a local downtown bar of one of her clients I decided to go. I resolved to move on and get out there—I missed my friends.

Sara and I were drinking like crazy, and for the first time in a month, I was having fun. A man in a suit looked interested in me and so I latched on. He was from Turkey and a current fellow at Mayo Clinic. I couldn't tell if he was cute and a little chunky or if he just seemed cute because I was drunk. *I won't be sure until I get him into bed.* The alcohol was playing with my mind and I started laughing. *I'm not going to bed with him! What is wrong with me?* I wondered how he would be as a lover. Probably not very good because I didn't think men from Turkey cared much about women—*nice follow-up from my last two men. Maybe a rebound would be good for me.* And I giggled, thinking about how I wanted to travel to Turkey.

He was staying in one of the downtown hotels, so we clumsily walked out the back door of the bar into the dark alley. Laughing and leaning against him, I saw a big man and two other guys walking our way. I couldn't see if it was Sam, but I knew it was. As they passed us, Turkey kept saying stupid shit and laughing, the same stupid shit I would have been giggling about if I hadn't just seen Sam. *Shut up! Shut up!*

Sam laughed sarcastically as he passed me. I sobered up quickly and I didn't want to be with Turkey. *What did Sam's laugh mean? Did he know it was me?* I didn't know what to do. I had to get rid of Turkey. How could I get rid of Turkey? I walked him back to his hotel room trying to figure out a way to leave him there. Once inside his room, I nervously said, "Oh my God, I forgot my keys! Sara has my keys in her purse! Crap! I'll be right back!"

"No. You stay here with me and get keys tomorrow," he said and stepped in my path.

"No, I need my keys. I won't be able to get my car or get into my apartment."

"I won't let you go," he said and stood in front of the door.

Oh my God, I have a crazy one. "I have to get my keys."

"I go with you."

"No, it will be faster if I just go. I'll be right back."

"You are leaving and you will not come back."

"Of course I'm coming back! I'll be right back!" I looked around, then kicked off my shoes. "I'll leave my shoes so you know I'm coming back. I'll be right back!" Barefoot, I darted for the door and escaped. I ran down the hall to the elevator and straight out the front doors. I ran down the sidewalk and into the bar hoping I wouldn't step on glass. I searched for Sam. I looked everywhere. I stood outside the men's bathroom and waited. I went out the back door to check the alley. I went back in and saw one of the guys who had come in with Sam. I grabbed him by the arm, and asked, "Where's Sam?"

"I think he left."

"Oh," I said as I sighed in disappointment. "Okay, thanks."

I found Sara and asked her if she saw Sam.

"What? No. Where is he?"

"I guess he left."

She draped herself over my shoulders and slurred, "That's good. Here have a shot."

"Sara, I have to go. Are you fine getting home?"

"Yes, my neighbor is here. She's the designated driver." She burst out laughing, and yelled, "Where are your shoes?" then decided to take off her shoes, too. She tried to sit on the floor to remove her shoes but I pulled her back up and wouldn't let her.

I found Sara's neighbor to make sure she was okay to drive, and she was, so I waited outside for a cab. The driver was a shabby looking older woman and as soon as she said, "Where to?" I told her I wanted to drive by my old boyfriend's house.

"I don't think that's a good idea."

"I know," I said and started crying. "I'm a wreck. He broke up with me a month ago. Then tonight I saw him for the first time. I was leaving the bar with a different man, a man I was planning on having sex with, I guess to try to help me move past Sam. But then I saw Sam so I... Oh God, it's a long story. I don't know what I'm doing. I left that guy and ran back to the bar barefoot to try to find Sam but he was already gone. I just want to drive by his house. I won't do anything crazy. I mean maybe I could ring his bell if his car is home... but what if he isn't alone? Ugh! I just want to drive by, that's it. Just drive by."

"Okay, honey. Where does he live?"

"Go north on Broadway."

"Just to let you know, I have power locks and I'm not going to let you out of the car."

"Promise?"

She laughed. "I've been in your shoes... oh that's right, you're not wearing any." She laughed again. "Let me tell you something from experience. If you find yourself acting like this, borderline stalking, he isn't the right guy. And if you're looking for another man to help you get over a man, you need to be alone for a while. It's as if you're trying to put out a fire with more fire. It don't work."

"I just want a glimpse of him... or his car or his place. Maybe I just need to find a way to say goodbye."

When we pulled up in front of Sam's apartment, I saw his car and knew he was home. I asked her if we could just wait. I sat in the back seat and cried, with my heart aching, and I didn't know what to do. I tried to do what everybody says to do—feel the pain, walk through the pain. So I sat there for fifteen minutes and cried, but again, I wasn't crying for Sam, I was crying about something much deeper. I was still a miserable person. I didn't know who I was or what I wanted. Logically, I knew Sam was wrong for me but being alone again was painful. I didn't want to be with myself—I didn't like myself.

When the cab driver dropped me off at home, she got out of the car and gave me a hug. "You'll get through this. You'll be okay." She stepped away, saying, "You're a good girl, and he's a fool for letting you get away." She got back into her car. "Don't sleep with strangers you meet in bars, honey. Okay? It won't help."

"Okay," I said and started laughing. "You're right. Thank you."

Chapter 12

MONDAY AFTER WORK, I found a note on my windshield from Sam. It said, *I've been thinking about you.* Everything inside of me screamed stay away, but I walked toward the deli anyway and saw him standing outside smoking a cigarette. When he turned and saw me, he rushed over to me and we embraced. He lifted me up and we kissed like no time had passed. I knew what I was doing. I was like a junkie trying to quit, knowing the stuff was bad for me. *Just give me a fix, just one little fix, then I'll be fine. Just one quick fix to regain my strength then I'll quit for good. Just one fix.*

"Are you done with work?" I asked.

"Just about, I need to close up and I want you to help me," he said and smiled.

"Okay, tell me what to do," I said as we walked into the deli and I set my bag down on one of the tables.

"Here." He handed me a rag and some disinfectant spray.

I started wiping down the tables, and he went in the back and turned up the music. *Crash Into Me* was playing. He locked the door and turned off the neon Open sign. He grabbed me from behind, and I could feel his hard heat pressing against my back. He led me into the backroom and started kissing me and caressing my breasts.

He pressed me against the counter and lifted my skirt. He picked me up and I pulled myself onto the countertop. He slipped between my legs and we both finished quickly. We held onto each other quivering. I started crying, but this time from the unease of having Sam back in my life.

We tidied ourselves up and I finished wiping down the tables while he counted the money for the deposit. I turned all the chairs and stools onto the tables and counters, before I headed back to wipe down our sex spot with disinfectant spray. He got the mop and bucket and quickly mopped the floor. We were a good team, working quickly because we both wanted to get out of there.

We drove to my apartment and had the place to ourselves. We didn't talk about what had happened or why we broke up. We just picked up where we left off, enjoying each other with no pressure to talk, no lectures about where we were going from here. I just wanted to be with him. I didn't want to be alone.

"I didn't sleep with that guy," I said.

"The guy in the suit? I know."

"Your friend told you?"

"I saw you in the cab outside my place. I was at the gas station next door getting milk. "

"Oh." I was embarrassed, feeling like a stalker.

He pulled me to him. "I didn't sleep with anybody either," he said, giving me a little squeeze. "Why didn't you call me?" he asked.

"I just don't want any pressure." I started playing with his hand. "I thought we were tired from the trip because it had been emotional for both of us, and I figured we needed a little space but I never dreamed a month would pass before one of us would give in. I guess once we hit the one month mark of not talking, I figured it was over and I needed to move on."

He laughed, and said, "With a drunk foreigner from a bar?"

I laughed, too. "The truth is, Sam, I'm a mess. I don't know who I am or what I want and it makes having a relationship difficult. I'm sorry I'm putting you through it."

He pushed himself against me for round two.

The next morning, we overslept because I'd forgotten to set the alarm clock. I barely made it to work on time and the rest of my day was just as crazy. Several clients who had been on the same cruise were unhappy. The ocean had been rough and they'd been sick, from food poisoning or sea sickness, they didn't know. But either way, they felt they deserved a discount on another cruise.

After a quick lunch with Sam, a man stepped into the office a little after two. He stared at me for a few seconds and then said, "I wait for you. You are a bitch!" and he left.

Sara turned and looked at me, then burst out laughing. "Turkey?"

"I guess." I shrugged my shoulders. "He was cuter than I thought, but chubbier too."

"Like a big Turkish teddy bear," she said and we both laughed.

"I wish he would have brought my sandals."

"Poor guy. You got his hopes all up that he might score with American blond woman."

"I'm not blond... and he might have if I hadn't seen Sam."

Sara kept laughing. "That was a fun night, well for me anyway. We have to do it again," Sara said. "I know you're back with Sam, but I could use some fun and maybe some help finding a man."

"Anytime." I turned to answer my phone. "Probably another disappointed client... Streamline Travel, this is Amanda."

Finally, a happy client. My best clients were an older married couple who traveled often and in style. They'd had the twenty-thousand dollar suite on the cruise. And they had a wonderful time. She said the rocking of the ship soothed her to sleep every night, and they had the best cruise ever so they were anxious to start planning their next.

"Amanda, you have got to go on a cruise! They are the best," she said.

"I know, you're right. I will one of these days. I'm so glad you had a great time. Next time you're downtown, stop by with pictures," I said before hanging up the phone. I had wanted to take a cruise for as long as I'd worked in the travel industry and I was envious of my clients and the people who could afford to travel so well. I dreamed of traveling, and working at the agency only emphasized my dreams. I wanted to travel the world and experience new places. I wanted to see everything.

I had been secretly saving money for years for my children. Even when I wasn't working and Nick was giving me an allowance, I was stashing away money. When it was obvious I wouldn't be able to have children and the divorce was inevitable, that money became a safety net for me. Originally, I thought I would use the money to go back to school, but the idea of traveling was so appealing to me now. I had asked my single brother, Teddy, to take a trip with me right after my divorce and starting my job with the travel agency, but he said I wasn't his ideal travel partner and with an attitude like that he wasn't mine either. So I just kept saving my money, daydreaming about traveling and waiting for the right travel partner.

I wasn't sure how Sam would fit in with my traveling dreams because he had a lot on his plate. His mom was getting older and he had a daughter to worry about. I knew that any extra money he had was going to help his family. I admired him but wondered if he would try to fit into my dreams.

That night, I spent at Sam's place and, over a dinner of fish sticks and macaroni and cheese, I asked him how he felt about traveling. "Where is your dream vacation spot?"

"We were just there. Anytime I spend with my family and friends, and time with my daughter is my dream vacation."

"But don't you ever want to get on a plane and fly over the ocean?"

"Never thought about it."

"Well, you should think about it because I want a travel partner. What do you think about the Cayman Islands? There are some great deals and I've always wanted to go there. They say the water is the most beautiful and the beach, Seven-Mile Beach, is nothing but fine white sand. What do you say? My treat. Are you in?"

"I don't think so. I just took a few days off and I need to work. I need the money."

"I understand, but think about it. How about Duluth, have you been there? It's beautiful. You could meet my parents. I know you're excited about that," I teased.

He shook his head and grinned back. "You're something," he said dismissively.

"Merging, this is called merging," I said, kissing him on the forehead. "I go your way, and you come my way." I was not going to let Sam become another Nick. I didn't want another one sided relationship.

He got up to clear the table, and quickly slapped my butt.

"Ouch! That hurt!"

"That's right. I need to keep you in line," he said and grinned.

"Give me a break."

Sam lunged at me pretending he was going to hit my butt again.

I jumped back and turned. "You think you're so tough," I scolded, "but I could knock you on your ass so fast, you wouldn't even know what hit you."

"Sure you could," he said and laughed.

"Yes, I could!" I wasn't trying to be tough or cocky, but I knew that I could knock him down and his attitude was starting to piss me off.

"Not a chance."

"Oh, yes I can, and I'll bet you that Cayman Island trip."

"Fine."

We finished clearing the table and rinsing the dishes as I chanted about how excited I was to go to Grand Cayman. Even though Sam was a huge man, much bigger than my brothers, I knew a surefire way to knock a man down. I learned it by accident while wrestling with Teddy when I was younger. If Sam had met my brothers, they would have warned him. When we were younger, I had been Teddy and Rob's favorite party trick and a way for them to make some quick cash over the years. I had knocked down every single one of their high school friends and many from college, too.

I lay down on the living room floor and told Sam to step over me. He did. I grabbed his ankles and pulled my legs up between his legs and rested them against his upper thighs. I gave him a gentle nudge not meaning to really make him fall, only to prove my point that I could do it and to win the Cayman Island contest, but he lost his balance and down he went with a loud thud. He lay there for a second and I was worried I hurt him or his ego. I quickly sat up to make sure he was okay and he grabbed me and pulled me on top of him. He rolled us over and he rested what felt like all his weight on me. He aggressively and forcefully held my hands over my head against the floor. He kept his grip on my hands with one hand and he yanked at my pants with the other hand. I was helpless. He was pressing against me. I couldn't move. I waited as he pulled his pants open. I spread my legs and let him thrust in deeply. I came immediately. He sustained his forceful pushing against me. I was throbbing and moaning in desperation to keep going. He kept moving fast and hard and I came again. He pulled me up and turned me over entering me from behind. He grabbed my breasts and continued to pound me. He reached for my clitoris and I knew he was coming so I joined him for the third time.

I was trembling, weak and exhausted. That was the best sex of my life. I had never come more than once, ever. Sam seemed proud of himself and for good reason. Sam was a drug and I was an addict. I could never get enough of him.

He was breathing hard and asked, "If I told you everything about my past, everything about my life, would you stay with me?"

"Yes… I would," I lied. "If I told you all of my future dreams, everything I want, would you stay with me?"

"Yes."

Chapter 13

THE FOLLOWING FRIDAY at work, I booked our trip to Grand Cayman, our airline tickets and hotel, and I got a great deal. Assuming Sam didn't have a passport, I checked on how to expedite the process to get his passport within six weeks before we left on our trip. It was to be a surprise for his birthday, which was right around the corner. I wanted to wait but I needed him to get his passport, so I took him out for dinner as an early birthday present and I gave him the envelope with the tickets and information about Grand Cayman.

"I'm only giving you this because we have to get your passport," I said, handing him the envelope. "I'm so excited. We're going to have the time of our lives."

He pulled out the tickets then pushed them back inside the envelope. "I can't go."

Reaching for his hand, I said, "Yes, you can. I talked to your boss and he said it's not a problem. I checked into everything. It's perfect."

"Amanda!"

"What? What's wrong?" I said, panic rising in my chest. *Please don't tell me you're afraid to fly or fear the ocean. Please don't tell me you're a felon and can't get a passport. Please don't tell me you don't care enough to meet me halfway. Please don't spoil my traveling dreams.*

"You don't get it!"

"Get what?"

"I'm sorry you did this."

"I'm not. You deserve it. You work hard, so you deserve a little fun in the sun."

Slowly shaking his head, Sam put his napkin on the table, pushed his chair back and stood up.

"Don't leave!" I cried out.

"I have to go."

"Don't leave! Don't leave me."

He stopped but didn't turn back.

"Sam! Are you breaking up with me?" I stared at him in disbelief. "Again?"

He walked out.

"Sam! Please don't leave me! Come on!"

I told the server to get my bill and I'd be right back. I ran after him. I ran into the street and yelled for him, "Sam! Sam!" I looked in every direction and ran down the block in the direction I thought he would have gone. I couldn't find him. "Fu-uck!" I sat down on the curb and started crying. *How can I be so stupid?* How could I think a man so completely wrong for me would somehow fit into my life or my future dreams?

I wiped my eyes, trying to gain my composer before going back into the restaurant. I paid the bill and grabbed the envelope with the plane tickets and reservations to the Marriott Grand Cayman right on Seven Mile Beach. I was still crying as I walked to my car. I was done for good. I didn't care how good the sex was or how I didn't want to be alone. I would never go back. I'd finally had enough.

When I got home, I cried myself to sleep hugging the stuffed dog Danielle had given me. I knew I wouldn't hear from Sam because I knew how he operated, and I knew how I operated, too. I wouldn't call him. I needed to get over him and figure out why I was drawn to someone like him in the first place. Was it just simply because my marriage was so boring I wanted some drama in my life to wake me up? I didn't know, but I had some work to do.

The next weekend I went to Duluth to stay with Teddy, the chef. He fed me well and gave me a shoulder to cry on, promising not to tell Mom, Dad or Rob about Sam and the heartache he had caused me. "He didn't sound right, from the start," he said, chopping an onion. "What was the attraction? Kinda sounds to me like you had your taste of a bad boy… and a rebound."

"I don't think he was a rebound. I don't know what he was other than wrong for me." I took a sip of my margarita. "We were doomed to failure—too different with different future dreams," I said. "Have you ever had a bad girl?"

"I try to be the bad boy to them. It's more fun."

"You, a bad boy? I don't see it," I giggled.

"Yeah, I know. But it keeps me from getting hurt. I do the hurting."

"Sounds like you've been hurt."

"Yep, remember Trish? I guess she was my bad girl. I was crazy about her and she destroyed me."

"I remember."

"I was so glad when she moved away so I could get on with my life. Out of sight, out of mind," he said, opening the oven to check on the chicken.

"Would you take her back if she knocked on your door tonight?"

"In a heartbeat."

After a wonderful dinner and comforting conversation with my brother, I knew I would call Sam when I got back to Rochester.

Maybe just to tell him I cared about him, maybe I just needed closure.

The following Monday, I was ready to reach out to Sam. On my lunch break, I went to the deli but didn't see him. "Is Sam here?" I asked his boss.

"No, he quit."

My heart dropped. "No, he didn't."

"Yes, he did. Friday."

"Did he have another job?"

"I don't know, but I don't think so. I think he's headed back to Chicago."

On the walk back to my office, I pulled my cellphone from my purse and dialed his number. It was disconnected. When I got back to work, I told my boss I had to go. "I feel sick and I'm sure it's food poisoning," I said, bending over and holding my stomach. I grabbed my things and rushed to my car, then drove straight to Sam's. When I got to his apartment, the front door was open and two cleaning women and his landlord were inside. I asked the landlord where Sam was.

"He moved out."

"He left all his things?"

"No, this apartment is rented furnished. If you know anybody interested, let me know."

"Where did he go? Where did Sam go?" I demanded.

"He gave me a Chicago address to mail his deposit to because he was in a hurry to get out of here."

"Why?"

"I don't know."

"Okay, thanks."

"Tell your friends about the apartment."

I walked away numb. So I guess that's it. I'm left again with no answers. Exactly the same way I felt throughout our entire relationship.

Chapter 14

SEVERAL WEEKS LATER, I was on a plane, by myself, on my way to Grand Cayman. I had a window seat and the seat next to me was empty. *The seat would have been too small and uncomfortable for Sam, anyway.* I smiled, realizing that I could actually think about Sam without any real emotion. It was a good feeling. I was moving on.

I reached into my bag and pulled out my very first letter from a family in Minneapolis—a family I had sponsored.

After Sam left me at the restaurant, I kept thinking about Danielle, Danae and the way they lived. So while at work, I grabbed the phone book and started paging through the yellow pages. I found an organization where you can sponsor a needy family. After getting more information, I knew it was something I had to do. "I don't mean to be picky, but do you have any single moms with a daughter that I could sponsor?"

"Funny you should ask. We just started helping a single mother with two kids, a five-year-old daughter and a three-year-old son. They live in Minneapolis."

"That's perfect. Sign me up." I signed a two-year commitment, but I wanted to see it through as long as they needed the help or until the kids graduated from high school. It was important to me.

On the front of the card was a kitten and the words, Thank You. I opened the card and a photo fell onto my lap—a young mother with her two adorable kids. I smiled.

Dear Amanda, Thank you for sponsoring my family. The commitment you made and the money you send each month will help more than you can possibly know. I feel blessed and honored to have you as a part of our family. I will keep you updated every month on the kids and my own progress. I'm working to get my GED and then I want to continue school so I can get a good job and support my family by myself. Thank you again. Love Michelle, Samantha and Wesley.

I put the photo and card back into the envelope then held it to my heart for a moment before slipping it back into my bag.

The man one seat over kept making small talk with me. He was a jeweler and gave me his business card and a twenty-five percent off coupon for anything in the store owned by the company he worked for. I thought it might be nice to buy myself something as a reward for taking this trip and for working my way past Sam. The man's name was John, and he was handsome, probably close to my age, maybe a little on the short side, but close to average. *Everybody seems short compared to Sam.* He asked me if I had been to Grand Cayman before.

"No, first time."

"Let me show you around. Let me take you out for dinner."

"Sure, that sounds nice."

He gave me his cellphone number, and I told him my name and where I was staying. He said he'd be more than happy to drop me off at my hotel because he had a rental car waiting at the airport.

When we were beginning our descent, I stopped talking to John so I could look out the window and experience the ocean and Grand Cayman from the air. It was beautiful, more beautiful than I imagined. The water was a mixture of bright blue and turquoise. The island seemed smaller than I expected and I could see the beautiful beaches of Grand Cayman. It was a dream come true, but a lonely one.

A steel band playing island music serenaded us as we departed the plane and walked into the airport. The humidity and heat were welcoming because it was starting to get colder in Minnesota. As we waited in the immigration line together, John guided me through my first time using my passport and I became more and more excited about the vacation stretching before me.

He waited with me for my luggage. I had two bags and he had a small carryon, so it was pretty obvious he wasn't staying long. We put our bags into the trunk, then I walked to the passenger's side of the rental car to get in. "Are you driving?" he asked.

"No."

"Really?"

"I'm sorry, I don't want to drive." I opened the car door and started laughing. The steering wheel was on the wrong side.

John was leaning against the roof of the car on the passenger's side that should have been the driver's side. He started laughing, too. "You have beautiful eyes, Amanda."

I blushed as I walked around the car to get in on the correct passenger's side. "Do you smoke?" I asked, comparing him to Sam and Nick and everything I didn't like about them.

He opened the door for me. "No. Do you?"

"No," I said and got inside. He closed the door behind me.

He dropped me off at the hotel, just after one o'clock and told me he would pick me up at six for dinner. With the whole afternoon in front of me, I pulled out my bathing suit and went straight to the beach. I set my towel down on a lounge chair, walked into the cool blue ocean, and swam out far enough that I could cry without anybody knowing. I had to cry, I wanted to cry, but it wasn't out of sadness really. I was a little sad that I was on this trip alone. But most of the tears were because I was saying goodbye to a mess of a life: Nick, my marriage, Sam. I couldn't believe I was forty-one and not happy with myself, not content in my life. I shed some tears for that too. I thought about some of the things Nick had said to me when he wanted me out of his life. "You're a miserable person…" and the last words I heard from Sam were, "I have to go." Those words played over and over in my mind. There was something I could learn form those words. *I don't want to be miserable. I don't want to be so easy to walk away from. I want to mean something to somebody. I want to mean something to myself.*

I had always thought the word closure was corny when talking about relationships—when it's over, it's over. But now I understood the importance of truly saying goodbye. I had been confused about Nick, and it's the same with Sam. *Why did he move away?* I wanted some type of closure with all of it. *I don't want to be back with Nick or Sam. I don't want to try again. I don't want to believe that with the right person I could have kids. I don't want to continue punishing myself.*

Maybe closure is a gift I give to myself. My salty tears mixed with the salt water that felt healing and cleansing. *I do want to start fresh. I do want to be happy. I do want to figure out who I am. When I'm ready, I do want a great man in my life who is interested in me and my dreams, who will meet me half way.*

I walked along the powder sand wishing I was holding hands with someone special. Sam would have been out of place, uncomfortable everywhere I wanted to take him and everyplace I wanted to go. I couldn't imagine holding hands and walking on the beach with Sam. It would have been a disaster. I giggled in that thought as I tried to walk a little taller with my shoulders back and chest out.

My brother always told me that happiness was a choice, just like misery, and I wanted to find my happiness. I knew things were different and so much time had passed since I remembered being truly happy. I've had my moments here and there but to actually be happy,

excited about my life and thrilled to get out of bed every morning—
it's been a while.

"Thank you, God, for letting me take this trip and for making
me take it alone," I said as I looked out over the ocean. I sat down on
the beach and with a broken shell, I wrote Sam in the wet sand at the
edge of the water. I watched wave after wave take him out to sea.
Then I wrote Nick in the sand and watched the water take him away.
I paused before writing Babies. I cried until all traces had been
washed away. I wiped my eyes and stood up. I tried to smile as I
stepped back into the ocean and an overwhelming sense of peace
came over me as if God was telling me to let go. My body relaxed as
the sun warmed my face. *I'm going to let go.*

I saw another hotel with an outdoor bar, so walked up the beach
in that direction. Not bothering to brush the sand off my legs—after
all, I was in the Cayman Islands—I bellied up to the bar in my bikini
and ordered a strawberry daiquiri.

When the handsome Australian set the drink in front of me, he
said, "I need to see ID."

"You're kidding, right?"

"How old are you?" he asked.

"Forty-one."

"I think I'll have to follow you back to your room because I
don't believe you." He winked.

It kind of felt like he was making a pass at me. "I'm sorry, I can
go get it."

"No worries. But you owe me."

"Oh, I'm sorry. How much?"

"No, not like that." He gave me a mischievous smile and asked,
"Are you staying here?"

"No, I'm at the Marriott."

"No worries. Would you like to start a tab?"

"No, thanks, just this." I took a sip and could immediately taste the alcohol.

He set the register tape in front of me. "Whenever you're ready, love." He walked over to another guy waiting for a drink.

I slipped my fingers into my swimming suit top and pulled out the soggy five dollar bill. I straightened it out as I read how much I owed him.

"Oh, my God! Excuse me!" I motioned for the tan Australian's attention. "I guess you *will* have to follow me to my room. I don't have enough money."

He smiled. "You must be new to the island."

"Yes, I flew in a couple hours ago."

"I'll tell you what, I got this one, and you buy me a drink later."

"I can't tonight…"

"Not tonight, just later."

"Okay, it's a deal. Thank you."

"Bring plenty of money next time because your six-dollar drink was seven twenty US."

"Really? Oh, my God." I giggled. "Thank you for telling me."

"It's pretty expensive here, but worth it," he said, winking at me again.

I gulped down my drink wanting to get back to the beach before I had to start getting ready for my date. I left the five dollars on the bar, just in case I didn't make it back his way. The idea of meeting a new man or even just hooking up with somebody on this trip hadn't crossed my mind until this sexy Australian flirted with me. I haven't felt attractive, sexy or interesting for a long time, not even while I was with Sam. I figured the Australian bartender was a big flirt, nothing more, and I really wasn't interested. But John, the jeweler, might be a different story.

After spending another hour on the beach, swimming a little and thinking a lot while slightly buzzed, I went back to my room to start getting ready. I was actually excited because I was attracted to John. He was attentive, full of compliments, with a nice sense of humor.

He picked me up at six and we went straight to The Grand Old House. The restaurant was beautiful and the weather was perfect for sitting outside. We drank some wine and I had one of the most delicious fish dinners I'd ever had. After we finished eating we strolled down by the edge of deck overlooking the water. The deck was on top of rocks and there were lights shining up from under the water. The waves were splashing against the rocks and you could see huge fish swimming around. Even though he had seen it before, he let me take my time enjoying our surroundings.

Before he drove me back to my hotel, he drove by the jewelry store where I could use my coupon. "Just look around and see if there's anything you would like."

"I will. I think I'll walk around Georgetown tomorrow and do some browsing."

"I have to work all day tomorrow, but I'd love to take you out again. Unfortunately, I won't have time to show you around during the day, but I can give you some pointers."

"Well, what do you suggest?"

"Take a tour out to Stingray City and do some snorkeling. Do you dive?"

"No."

"Okay, then maybe do the glass-bottom boat, too. It's worth the money. And you might want to rent a car and drive around the island. It's beautiful and safe. Just remember to stay on the left. Get a map from the hotel but you can't get too lost, right? It's an island." He parked the car in the hotel parking lot and reached for my hand, kissing my palm. "You are very beautiful."

"Thank you." I felt butterflies in my stomach and I was trying to figure out how to keep the date going. I wanted to kiss him. "I think I might take a little stroll on the beach. Do you want to join me?"

"Sure, I'd love to."

We slipped off our shoes before stepping onto the sand, and he held my hand as we walked along the waves. We stopped and kissed, and then he led me away from the water and we sat on the beach. John was easy to be with and very gentle while holding my hand and kissing me. We leaned back onto the sand and made out. He never attempted more than pressing against me, kissing me and a few brushes against my breasts. "Do you want to come to my room?" I whispered.

"Are you sure?"

"Yes, but I don't have any protection."

"I do."

We held hands and made our way back to the car where he had a bag in the console. I knew he was a fling and I'd probably never see him after this trip, but I didn't care. We went to my room and closed the door. He became slightly more aggressive and so did I. We played around for what seemed like an hour, taking our time holding, touching and caressing one another. I slipped the condom on him and we made love slowly and sensually. John was a good lover, but very different than Sam.

It was a satisfying night and even better when John said he should get going. I didn't want him to spend the night. I wanted to enjoy the hotel room alone. That night I slept well and had sweet dreams—I was in the Cayman Islands.

The phone woke me the next morning, it was John telling me he'd had a wonderful night and could he take me out for dinner again. "Of course," I said and smiled at the memory of the night before.

"Tonight, Lobster Pot. Six o'clock?"

"Sounds good. I'll see you then." I rolled out of bed and skipped the shower. I slipped into my bathing suit and the sundress I had worn the night before. The beach wasn't busy, a few walkers and some hotel staff setting up chairs. I dived in and went for a long, refreshing swim in the ocean. When I finished, my arms felt like rubber and I needed a coffee, so I sat down at the hotel restaurant. "What can I get for you, love?"

I recognized his accent and looked up from the menu. Sure enough, it was my Australian flirt from the other hotel bar. "You work here, too?"

"Yes. When are you going to buy me that drink?"

"I'm not sure, but I will before I go."

"Well, just for your information, I'll be here the rest of the week," he said.

"So will I. But for now, I need a coffee, raspberry mocha if you have it."

"One raspberry mocha, coming up. I'm assuming this will be a room charge?"

"Yes."

"Room number?" he asked with his mischievous smile.

"Um, I guess I better pay with cash," I teased back and gave him my room number.

"You're so forward, practically pushing your room key in my pants," he said, winked and walked away.

"Oh, can I get the mocha to go."

"You got it."

Chapter 15

AFTER I SHOWERED and dressed, I called a cab and made a reservation for the glass-bottom boat. John was right; the underwater boat was awesome. Even though I had moments of sadness because I was alone, I also had moments of pride in myself for doing it alone.

There were three big cruise ships sitting at port, and I started daydreaming about going on a cruise. *Someday, maybe my next trip.* Filled with hope, I continued my walk toward the Georgetown shops and the jewelry store John worked for. I didn't have much jewelry: a ring that belonged to my grandma that I never wore; a cross necklace that I got for confirmation that I wore for special occasions; and diamond earrings that I got from my dad that I always wore. Since the day he gave them to me when I was sixteen, I never wanted any other earrings and I never took them off. I liked jewelry, but I wasn't sure I'd buy anything because I didn't budget for extra spending and I had forgotten about the dollar difference. I did have the money, but I didn't want to go through all of it on one trip. If I was going to get something, it would have to be a necklace and it would have to be spectacular.

I browsed through a perfume store, a few tourist shops and clothing stores. I avoided all the jewelry stores until I found John's

and stepped inside. I started on one side of the store with every
intention of seeing everything the store had to offer before I made a
decision. About half way through, I had three necklaces on my
maybe list, but nothing spectacular and I hadn't checked the prices
yet, so I kept searching.

I was thankful that the store was busy with cruise ship passengers. The traffic kept the salespeople busy so I was free to look without pressure. I glanced around the store and wondered if any of the
people from the ships were my clients. Sometimes the entire transac-
tion was done via email, fax and phone and I didn't get to see the
people I was sending on beautiful vacations.

"Miss, can I help you?"

"No thank you," I said, and turned to tell the man, "I'm just
look…" It was John. "Um, yes, sir, you can help me. I'm looking for
a necklace, something that will always remind me of my amazing trip
to the Cayman Islands."

"I see," he said with his hand on his chin. "You look like somebody who would like something elegant and delicate, nothing big and
gaudy, that's not you. Am I right?"

"You're right." I smiled.

"I'm thinking a pendant on a petite gold chain."

"That sounds nice."

"Okay, follow me. Now, the chain isn't the issue, let's find the
pendant first. I just happened to set aside a few I thought somebody
like you might like. We have this Australian Opal that just happens to
be the same color as the ocean on Seven Mile Beach."

I bought the first one he showed me, a tiny heart made of
Australian Opal encased in gold. It was spectacular and fit every part
of my trip so far: I was trying to heal my heart, the necklace reminded
me of John, and the color of the stone perfectly matched the water
off Seven Mile Beach, not to mention it was Australian like my bar-
tending flirt. John matched it with the perfect fourteen-inch, gold,

feminine but strong chain, and I put it on before I walked out of the store. I had spent only about a hundred dollars US because John gave me a great deal on top of the twenty-five percent off coupon I used. And it felt great, resting just between my collarbones in that little dip.

I decided to skip the cab and walk back to the hotel. It wasn't that far, maybe a couple miles, and the walk would be good for me. The car traffic was heavy close to downtown, which made me a little nervous. I hoped it would lighten up further down the road or at least there would be a consistent sidewalk to walk on. The cars driving on the left also made me nervous, so I walked cautiously, but let my mind race with thoughts about John. All I knew was that he worked with jewelry and was from Texas, without the Texan accent. Our talks hadn't revealed much about each other and my thoughts went from one extreme to the other. First, I feared he was married, then I feared he would want to have a relationship with me. I hoped he didn't think the heart pendant had to do with love or me wanting to find love.

By the time I made it back to the hotel, feeling stressed by the wild traffic whizzing by me, I wanted a drink. I headed straight to Hemmingway's bar and searched out my Aussie, but he wasn't there. Sipping a glass of wine and listening to the soft music playing, I started to feel better, just a little tired. I wondered if I had time for a powernap, so I asked the bartender for the time.

"Just after four."

"Can I take this glass to my room?"

"Sure. Room charge right?"

"Oh, here," I wrote down my room number and signed the tab. "Thanks."

When I got back to my room, I called the front desk for a wake-up call in forty minutes and I crashed hard. I dreamed about Sam but felt refreshed and happy when I woke up to the phone ringing. At first, I had no idea where I was. *I love when that happens.* I turned on the clock radio and island music was playing. I turned it up, took a sip of wine and jumped in the shower.

At six, John was at my hotel room door. He had flowers for me and gave me a tender kiss. "Want to stay in?"

"I'd love to but I'm starving." I giggled.

"Well then, let's get you fed." He smiled, adding, "By the way, I love your necklace."

"Thanks, me too." I smiled and reached for the heart. I rubbed my finger against the smooth opal. "Thanks for your help and for the deal."

"I didn't give you a deal. Do you have any idea how high we bump the prices?"

I laughed. "Well, thank you anyway. You have no idea how perfect this necklace is for me right now."

"You can tell me all about it over dinner."

The Lobster Pot was a little more casual than The Grand Old House, but it was nice and the food was amazing. We both ordered the trio—lobster, fish and shrimp. We sat by the window watching the large tarpon splashing around looking for food.

"So tell me what that necklace means to you."

"Oh, well, it's a long story." I took a sip of my wine. I was afraid if I started to open up, I wouldn't be able to stop. I didn't want to share too much. "So, when do you head back to Texas?"

"Well, I was supposed to go back tomorrow but I extended my trip another day."

Oh no, here we go.

"I was hoping I could see you again tomorrow night."

"You're spoiling me."

He looked into my eyes, then looked down. "I think you're beautiful and I like spending time with you."

Translation: You like the sex—which is fine because I do, too.

"As you know, I do take trips to the Minneapolis region and I would like to see you again, after this trip."

"Really?" I didn't expect that. "I'm… I'm in a weird place right now. And I know this is going to sound crazy but I'm trying to find myself. I lost her a long time ago." I felt a little choked up saying it out loud. *Plus, we live in different states. It could never work so why can't we just enjoy this time we have together?*

"Amanda, you're just so easy…"

I burst out laughing.

"No, you didn't let me finish. Amanda. You're easy," he smiled, "to be with."

The truth was I felt the same way about him. From what I could tell, John was a good catch. He was easy to be with and I kind of liked myself while I was around him. *Maybe I shouldn't close this door.* "I don't know what to say."

"No pressure, I'd just like to exchange phone numbers and see what happens."

"I can do that."

"Can I tell you something?" he asked and looked around quickly. Leaning toward me, he said, "I've been rock hard for the last hour. I'm glad we skipped dessert. It's not easy sitting across the table from you."

I smiled and felt a rush in my stomach. John made me feel beautiful and sexy and interesting. I was suddenly aroused myself. "Let's get out of here." We hurried to the hotel and had a repeat of the night before. This time we had pillow talk before he decided to get up and go. It was funny because, this time, I didn't want him to leave.

I was in familiar territory with this war going on inside of me wanting him and not wanting him at the same time, analyzing and trying to figure out if he would be a good fit in my life. I knew we had only a short time to get to know each other and I had a hard time believing long-distance relationships worked, but I wanted to see what would happen.

When John left, it was only ten-thirty and I was feeling antsy. I got dressed again and strolled down to the bar for another glass of wine. As I stepped into Hemingway's, I heard somebody yell my name. It was Steve, the Australian, and he was sitting at a table with two other guys and a girl. "Amanda, over here!"

I joined them and said, "What can I get you to drink?"

"I'll take a shot of tequila, but you have to have one, too," he said.

At the bar, I ordered five shots, five limes and a salt shaker, then rejoined the others at the table. The heavy guy roared, "Body shots!"

"Not a chance," I said quickly.

Steve made room for me to sit next to him. "Ready?" He licked the salt from his hand, slammed the shot, then sucked on the lime. "Your turn!"

I took my shot and my throat was on fire. I hadn't done a shot of tequila for months and, within fifteen minutes while sipping on a beer, I was feeling my liquor. I knew I should go to bed, but I was having fun and I was on vacation. I liked Steve and his friends but I felt old and ridiculously out of place. When Steve started putting his hand on my thigh, it was time to go back to my room. His hand moved further up my thigh and I jumped to my feet. "I gotta go. Goodnight. It was nice meeting all of you and I hope we can do it again before I go."

Steve stood up and said, "I'll walk you to your room."

"No, that's okay."

"I'll be right back," he said to the guys at the table.

When we were in the secluded hallway in front of my hotel room door, I felt uncomfortable and I wanted him to walk away before I took out my room key.

"I'm sorry I put my hand on your leg. I have a girlfriend. I shouldn't have done that. Please don't tell anybody. I know I'm a big flirt and I don't mean anything by it. I think you're really nice and I know you're older, but you look really good. You know that, right? You're sexy, and if I didn't have a girlfriend..."

"That's nice of you to say, but I have a boyfriend, too," I lied. "So I'm not going to tell anyone."

"Okay. Well, I better get back. Hug?" He opened his arms and leaned forward. He held on too long. "Oh, you feel good..." He started rubbing his arms up and down my back.

"Knock it off!" I pushed him back and started laughing.

"Okay, truce." He laughed and put his hand out. "Let's shake on it."

I reached for his hand.

"Oh, that's nice..." he said and closed his eyes while rubbing his thumb across my hand.

"Very funny. Goodnight."

He pulled my hand to his mouth and stuck out his big, wet tongue and licked my hand and kept licking up my arm.

I wiped off my arm and hand. "That's disgusting! Get out of here!" I said, amused.

Laughing, he turned and walked down the hall. "See you tomorrow," he said as he turned back around and kept walking backward. "Mocha in the morning?"

"Yes," I said as I unlocked my door. "Goodnight."

"Goodnight, Amanda."

I giggled as I stepped into my room. So far, this trip has been good for me. I'm far from perfect, but I haven't smiled this much in a long time. I glanced at my reflection in the mirror and my shoulders were back, I was standing up straighter. I stared at myself and a tear gently rolled down my cheek.

Chapter 16

THE NEXT MORNING I went for a swim, then to see Steve for my raspberry mocha to go. I decided to take John's advice about renting a car to see the island. When I got to the blowholes, I stopped and sat down on a bench to watch the ocean waves push through the rocks. It was beautiful.

Here I sat on a bench in Grand Cayman alone. I thought about the choices I was making and I didn't know if I wanted to start another relationship so soon. A huge wave hit the rocks and shot high into the sky. I reached for my necklace and rubbed my finger against the stone. For some reason, I didn't think John was right for me and it went deeper than just the distance between us. It was a gut feeling. I continued watching the blowholes knowing I would still explore the possibility of a long-distance relationship and I would give him my phone number, but I would pay attention to my instincts. Besides, it might be nice to talk to him once in a while, and to take a short trip to the cities to spend time with him. I liked him.

Smiling, I stood up and walked back to the car. I had to get back to the other side of the island for the last trip out to Stingray City around three o'clock. Then John had something special planned for our date.

Stingray City was not what I expected. It wasn't a city, just a sandbar in the ocean where stingrays came to feed. I met some great couples who were on cruises, and the nearby snorkeling was astounding; I could have stayed under the water with the fish and stingrays all day. That was definitely my favorite part of the trip so far.

At precisely six o'clock when John knocked on my door, I was ready for our date. "Hi, John. My heart is racing," I said, and reached for his hand to place it on my breast. "See."

"That's not your heart."

"Well, close. Do you feel it?" I said and smiled.

Not letting go of my breast, he started kissing me, holding one breast in each hand. We moved to the bed and had a quick fulfilling romp. I figured now we wouldn't be rushed at dinner because tonight, I did want dessert. And I wanted to spend the time getting to know him.

We drove to a marina and he pulled a picnic basket out of the car. We walked up to a small yacht and the captain greeted us. "I'm sorry we're late," John said.

"No problem."

I giggled to myself. *Whoopsy.*

We took off our shoes, and the captain placed them in a basket.

"This is my boss's yacht. I told him what I had going on down here and he set this up for us."

If he was telling people about us, this was more serious than I thought. Turning toward him, I reached for his hands. "Thank you, this is a wonderful surprise." I gave him a hug.

"We're just taking an evening cruise around the island, so it'll take a few hours. Right, Captain?"

"That's right," he said as he brought the shoe basket on board. "You two relax, take a look around. I have to do a few things to get ready, then we should be leaving in about ten minutes. It's a calm night, no rough seas, but there is an area getting out of the reef that's always a little rough, but that will only last about ten or fifteen minutes. I'll warn you before we get there. Can I get either of you anything right now?"

"Not for me," John said and turned to look at me.

"I'm fine, too, thanks."

John and I dug into the picnic basket. He poured each of us a glass of wine and pulled out some grapes and cheese. After doing a quick tour of the yacht, we settled in on the aft deck next to our picnic basket.

"How old are you?" I asked.

"Forty-one."

"What's your status?"

"Divorced."

"Oh, divorced." I didn't expect that. "Why?"

"Married young, grew apart. Mutual. Still get and give Christmas cards. That's the extent of it."

"Divorced how long?"

"Eight years."

"How many long-terms since the divorce?"

"Two."

"What happened?"

"Just not right."

"Why don't you have a Texan accent?"

"I'm originally from California, and just moved to Texas three years ago. I guess I never picked it up."

"Hmmm…" I took a sip of wine. "Kids?"

"Not yet," he said and smiled.

And there it was. That was what my gut was telling me. John was a man in search of a family. I felt like I'd been stabbed in the heart. I took a deep breath. "John, I'm forty-one also and I can't have kids."

"Forty-one?" He laughed nervously. "Wow, I'm a little, well, shocked. Forty-one? You look young. I thought you were younger but you're healthy, I'm sure you can still have kids. We'll just have to hurry." He said with a defeated smile.

"I'm divorced, too. I can't have kids." I didn't lower my head like I was defective or sorry. I looked him in his eyes.

It felt like he was about to tell the captain to hold everything. I became nervous, because it seemed he thought he had made a terrible mistake. He appeared to completely lose interest in me. "I really want children."

Instead of telling him about all the pain I'd gone through, I swallowed the lump in my throat and just said, "You're a great guy and you should have children." I took a deep breath. "I understand. I used to want children, badly. But I've come to terms with it and I don't want children anymore."

He went quiet so I stood up and walked to the railing while the yacht began moving out of the marina and into the north sound. It was a beautiful evening. Just when I was getting used to the idea of giving John and a long-distance relationship a try, my gut proved to be right. *That's amazing.* I turned around and looked at him. "I'm sorry.

"I'm sorry, too, Amanda." He stepped next to me, held my hand and said, "I want children."

"It's okay. I understand and I don't blame you at all." I smiled. "I guess we're just not a good fit, but I sure had a nice time with you. You deserve to have what you want. I was a little concerned about a long-distance relationship anyway."

He smiled but said nothing. He wrapped his arms around me. I could feel his manhood pressing against my hip. "You're right about the long-distance thing."

"I know."

"Oh, Amanda." He gave me a squeeze. "I was so sure about us. I was planning our wedding and our life, I envisioned us having two children and growing old together," he said, facing me. "I promised my boss I wouldn't, but I really want to take you down to one of the staterooms right now and try to make a baby."

The captain interrupted telling us to move up front to see the flying fish, so holding on to the rails, we made our way to the big lounge pads. "There's a lot of flying fish in this area. Keep your eyes open and you'll see them. They look like birds," the captain said.

We watched and waited. "There's one," John said pointing. I didn't see anything. "There's another one! Two! Five!"

That time I saw them. "Oh, my God! They do look like birds!" I kept looking. "There's one!"

We stayed up front until it was too dark to see the flying fish, and then the captain told us to go back because we were approaching some rougher water.

John and I sat in back cuddling on the padded bench and looking at the island from a distance. The lights sparkled and the stars were shining. I could tell there had been a shift in the way he felt about me and I was okay with that; in fact, in some ways I was relieved.

Our beautiful cruise around Grand Cayman was unforgettable. I felt lucky to have met John because he had been a wonderful distraction, and a lesson. When we got back to my hotel room, we held each other through the night but we didn't make love and before John left we exchanged phone numbers and said our goodbyes. I went back to bed and woke to Steve knocking on my door holding a raspberry mocha. "Room service."

I opened the door, grabbed the mocha and got back into bed. He followed me and lay down at the foot of the bed.

"Your man leaves today, huh?"

"Yeah."

"Are you sad?"

"I don't think so."

"He's not the one, is he?"

"I don't think so."

"Maybe I'm the one."

"I don't think so."

He smiled. "Are you going for your swim?"

"Yes, I'm spending the day on the beach, so keep the drinks coming," I teased.

"I'll keep an eye on you." He stood up. "You want breakfast? I'll bring it up to you."

"Ya know, I'd love some scrambled eggs and toast."

"No worries. I'll be right back."

I snuggled with a pillow and looked forward to a day to myself. I was glad John was leaving, probably on the plane at that very moment. The rest of my trip would be mine and mine alone. I was getting more comfortable being alone.

Steve delivered my breakfast order and said they were getting busy downstairs. He told me the hotel was having a beach party with live music that night and I should come. He said he had to work and would be busy, but some of his friends would be happy to keep me company. I told him I'd see how the day played out.

After breakfast, I packed my beach bag with sunscreen, a novel, a towel, fashion magazines, chapstick, money, the room key and a bottle of water. I planned to spend the day at the beach—swimming, walking and relaxing—so I set up my chair, got comfortable and gazed out at the endless ocean. I was calm and content, watching the waves. I closed my eyes and fell asleep.

Steve woke me and was holding a drink with an umbrella, a strawberry daiquiri. "John called. This is from him." He set the glass on the table next to me. "He told me to tell you he had a wonderful time, and he's thinking about you."

I smiled, then reached for my necklace and rubbed the heart.

"Who's your heart-on for? Me?" Steve asked.

"I thought it was for an ex but maybe I have a heart-on for me."

"I like it."

"Thanks."

"Let me know if you need anything."

"Okay." I sipped on my straw, then started playing with the umbrella. I remembered my parents giving me their drink umbrellas to play with when I was a little girl. *I should probably call them. I'll call everybody tonight to let them know I'm fine.*

When I started getting hot, I went for a swim. I stayed parallel to the beach but swam as far as I could, then walked back along the water's edge. I could feel the sun on my skin and hoped my sunscreen was waterproof. When I got back to my chair, I reapplied sunscreen and read a few chapters from my novel before I started watching people playing in the water and walking along the shoreline. I noticed that a lot of people were walking alone on the beach and that made me feel less alone.

Chapter 17

THE REMAINDER OF my vacation was filled with long-distance swims and walks on the beach, browsing through shops, and eating at a variety of restaurants; Ragazzi and the Lobster Pot were my favorites. I didn't drink another drop of alcohol since John's strawberry daiquiri and I skipped all the invites from Steve.

When I landed in Minneapolis, I was tan, refreshed and feeling excited about getting back on track with saving money for another trip, alone or not. I wanted to travel. I drove back to Rochester in a typical October snowstorm, forcing me to acclimatize quickly to the northern environment. When I got home, a note from Teresa was on the table: *Welcome home! I can't wait to hear all about it! I didn't want to tell you like this, but I think Sam has been calling here. He won't leave a message. See you soon! T*

My heart skipped a beat. *I don't care. I don't want to hear it.* I started unpacking my suitcase, trying to ignore the note. I turned on the stereo, threw in a load of laundry, gathered up the drycleaning and put my toiletries away in the bathroom. I set my alarm clock and got ready for bed because I planned to go into work early. I knew I'd have a lot of work to catch up on.

I didn't sleep well, tossing and turning and wanting to hold onto my Cayman Island good feelings while back in Rochester.

The morning came too early. I showered and went straight to Starbucks for a large raspberry mocha. First in the office, I placed the newly framed photo of my adopted family on my desk and started checking my phone messages. There were the expected messages along with several hang-ups. I turned on my computer and started checking my emails. I glanced up and saw a new poster of the largest cruise ship on the water, Oasis of the Seas. "That's my next trip," I said out loud.

I grabbed one of the brochures from Sara's desk and I stuck it in my purse, then drank down a few gulps of coffee. My workload wasn't as bad as I had expected, but I knew Sara would have some problems for me. I took my checkbook out of my purse and started figuring the damage of the last few months: my time with Sam and my Cayman trip.

We weren't open yet but my phone rang so I answered it.

"It's me," Sam said and cleared his throat.

I slammed the phone down and I was suddenly right back in the middle of every emotion, every feeling, every physical reaction of our turbulent relationship.

The phone rang again but I didn't answer it. "Fu-uck!"

I waited, then checked my messages. "I miss you, Amanda," was the message he left. The sincerity in his voice made tears well up in my eyes.

My heart was racing. *Okay. Okay, I can do this.* I settled down when Sara came in and I let her fill me in on everything I needed to know. I briefly told her about my trip. I left John out and only talked about the beautiful beach and weather. I said it was a trip of nothing more than sunshine, relaxation and time to myself. That's when she said she thought Sam might have called a couple of times.

"I forwarded him to your voicemail," she said.

"You know, I really don't care."

"Wow, that vacation was good for you."

Wanting to change the subject, I asked, "Hey, what are you hearing about the Oasis?"

By Friday, I was all caught up and wanted to work on Saturday for extra hours. If I was going to go traveling, I needed to get my bank account back to where it was before my Chicago and Cayman trips. James, who usually worked weekends, needed time off so it worked out perfectly.

I was the last to leave on Friday night. It was cold, dark and snowy outside and I dreaded the walk to my car. I gathered my things, put on my coat and looked outside when I saw Sam smoking a cigarette and walking toward the office, my knees went weak and I felt like I was going to collapse by my desk. My fling with John hadn't been a complete success.

The door was locked so he stood outside and waited. Stepping outside, I barely acknowledged him as I locked the door and started walking to the parking garage. "I thought you moved back to Chicago," I said.

"Yes, temporarily. My mom was sick."

I stopped and turned toward him. "Oh my God, is she okay?"

"Yes, she's better now." He walked with me with his hands in his pockets. "How was your trip?"

"Nice. You would have liked it."

He didn't say anything.

"I have to get going. I'm glad everything is fine with you and your family."

"Everything isn't fine," he said and grabbed my arm to stop me. "I miss you."

I faced him. "I'm not doing it again, Sam."

He reached up and touched my face. "Amanda," he said softly.

"Sam, don't!" I closed my eyes and reached for his hand. "Please, I have to go."

"Can we talk?"

Suddenly angry, I raised my voice, "Talk! Are you fucking kidding me? I didn't think you were capable of talking! You never talk! You don't talk!" I turned around away from him and shook my head in disbelief. "You want to talk? You really want to talk?" I turned back toward him.

"Yes, I want to talk."

"Okay, I'm listening. What do you have to say that is so important?"

"I love you."

"That's not enough, Sam. What else you got?"

"Let's go to your place so we can talk."

"No." I started walking to my car and he followed. When I was about to get in, he held my door closed so I couldn't.

"You have to give us a chance."

"Oh, you mean the way *you've* given us a chance."

"Amanda, wait!"

"What, Sam? What?" I couldn't control my tears.

"Let me spend the night with you."

I gave him the dirtiest look I could manage and opened the car door. "What do you want? What do you want, Sam?"

"I want you," he said and lowered his head.

"What would be different? What is different from when you walked away from me and left me at the restaurant holding two tickets to Grand Cayman?" I grabbed the front of his leather coat. "Tell me what has changed, what is different?"

"I don't know. I can't get over you. I still love you... the same..."

"Well then, maybe I'm different now. Maybe I've changed." I got into my car. He stepped back and let me drive away. When I looked in my rearview mirror, I saw him standing in the middle of the road, watching me drive away—it seemed like he was crying.

My heart dropped and I drove only a few blocks before I made a u-turn and went back to find him. I knew I wouldn't take him home with me, but I didn't want to hurt him. I didn't want to see Sam hurting. He was no longer there. I drove around the block and searched the alleys and side streets. I drove around downtown for twenty minutes, up and down the streets desperately wanting to find him before I gave up and went home.

Even though I hadn't heard from John since I returned to Rochester, I still had a sense that John was between Sam and me. If I hadn't been with John, I might have caved to Sam's sex. Another reason I was grateful for John. He was like a compass pointing me in a different direction.

Chapter 18

THE NEXT YEAR was one of working hard, saving money and living a quiet, boring life. The most exciting part of my life was spending time with my family and friends and receiving the monthly letter from my adopted family. Michelle had gotten her GED and received a grant to go to college. Samantha had started kindergarten and loved it. Unfortunately, Wesley, the little daredevil, fell off a six-foot fence and broke his arm. He was still in a cast but seemed to like the attention. All and all, things were going well for them.

Teresa got engaged and moved in with Jim. I kept the apartment, but didn't get a new roommate and enjoyed having the place to myself. To offset the extra rent, I turned Teresa's room into a gym with weights and a treadmill and ditched my gym membership. I cut out all the cable channels, keeping only the basic package, and I got rid of my home phone, keeping only my cellphone. I worked extra hours at the agency when they'd let me, and I took a part-time job working at a tanning salon some evenings and weekends. Each of the tanning rooms was named after a tropical island, and one of them was Grand Cayman.

I heard from both John and Steve a few times. John and I actually tried to plan a meeting in Minneapolis but his trip fell through and the calls became fewer. I heard rumors about Sam from time to time, and one of his friends called me once in a while to check in with me. He'd fill me in with what was happening with Sam, and I assumed he relayed my news back, but I wasn't sure. I didn't mind his phone calls because I liked hearing about Sam; it reminded me how much better my life was without him.

The worst was when I'd run into some of his friends at the bar while out with Sara or Teresa. They would tell me how fucked up I was, and laugh. "Sam would have done anything for you. Never seen a man so much in love… and in so much pain. You have no idea how much he loved you," they'd say. I didn't like hearing about Sam being hurt by me; we both had been hurt.

Teddy moved to Rochester from Duluth for a great catering job, and he had been a godsend when I really needed him. Even though I didn't go into great detail about my love life, he seemed to be the voice of reason I sometimes needed. He helped me through the moments I doubted myself, and it was nice to help him out occasionally, too. He had some relationship troubles of his own and we cured each other's lonely moments by going to the movies or out to eat. I loved having him so close.

After months of working hard and filling in wherever I was needed, I was promoted to office manager and had my own office space in the back. I cut back my part-time job at the tanning salon to Sundays only, and I started taking some online classes on tourism and travel. My goal was to eventually ask Streamline Travel to host my own travel agency. I was very excited about my future. My thrifty ways were paying off with a growing bank account and increasing vacation time, so I started making plans for a cruise on Oasis of the Seas. I found an amazing deal and booked it before I had a chance to second-guess myself. The cruise left in one month, right after Halloween, and I was looking forward to another trip. I had secretly hoped that I wouldn't still be alone for my next vacation, but I was fine going by myself. I was happy that I had no clients going on the same cruise. I didn't want to have to hide from unhappy people, and there were always some customers who were never happy.

I was ready to get out of Rochester for a while and sail into some tropical weather.

Chapter 19

AFTER A SMOOTH flight to Ft. Lauderdale and an easy shuttle ride over to Port Everglades, the ship's loading was chaotic. But I'd expected that because it was probably the number one complaint from my cruise ship clients.

I got to my room, a higher-end loft suite, loving the perks of being a travel agent. Before I left Rochester, I'd been able to book myself into a vacant high-priced room. I was spoiling myself but in some ways this was a working vacation, because I wanted to learn as much as I could about cruising so I could be better at my job. I'd be an undercover travel agent.

Waiting for my luggage to be delivered to my room, I explored the huge ship. I spotted the spa and gym first, then several restaurants, buffets and snack shops. I found the rock-climbing wall and water-show stage, the casino and ice-skating rink, and the dance and comedy clubs. I wanted to be on my deck when the ship left port, so I went back to see if my suitcase had been delivered.

I unpacked my bags, hanging my clothes in the closet and putting my makeup and shampoo in the bathroom. This would be my beautiful floating apartment for the next six days. With a Perrier from the mini bar, I sat outside on my deck waiting for the ship to sail. My suite deck faced aft, overlooking the basketball court, miniature golf course and surfing pools with a soon-to-be wonderful view of the ocean on either side. But until we left, I had to settle for the industrial buildings of Port Everglades.

There was an announcement over the intercom, something about a safety demonstration. I left my room and found a crewmember who explained how my room key indicated where to go for the drill and in case of an emergency. When I found my area, I sat at a table and watched the room fill with other cruisers, smiling and excited to be on a cruise.

An older woman with a cane was looking for a seat so I quickly stood up and offered her mine. I helped her sit down, then quickly searched the room for another chair and carried it over and set it next to her so her husband could sit down, too.

I noticed that most of the people were older—lots of grey hair in the room—but some were middle-aged and younger. Everybody seemed to be in a couple or with family, but I did see one nice-looking man who was by himself. I had seen him on the shuttle from the Lauderdale Airport, too. He was probably my age or a little older. I glanced around the room again before the safety film began. I couldn't stop smiling.

Paying little attention to the safety film, I mentally made plans for the rest of my day. I'd watch us leave the port, then go for a run on the track before having dinner at the buffet. In the evening, I'd catch one of the events and maybe take a peek inside the dance club. Maybe I'd even have a drink.

When the demonstration was over, I made my way through the crowd and back to my room on the seventeenth floor. As I was sticking my card in my door lock, I noticed the *single* man at the door next to mine. "Hi, neighbor," I said.

He smiled politely and nodded.

In my room, I laughed at my nerdiness and slipped off my shoes. When I stepped out onto the deck, the soothing music played throughout the ship, so I sat on the small couch, with my legs up on the coffee table, relaxed and waited for our departure.

The song changed and *Crash Into Me* started playing. That song always reminded me of Sam and the night I helped him close the deli. I closed my eyes and listened.

I heard glass break on the deck next to mine. "Shit!"

I knew I shouldn't but I couldn't help myself. "You okay?"

I heard his door slide shut as if he'd gone inside.

My neighbor was unfriendly and seemed to want to be left alone, but the more he ignored me, the more I wanted to talk to him. *Story of my life.* I had to stop. I took a deep breath and sipped my Perrier. As the boat started moving, I reached for my heart pendant, which brought back memories of John and our cruise around Grand Cayman.

I was startled by my neighbor peeking over to my side of the deck. "I'm sorry," he said. "I didn't mean to scare you. I dropped a bottle and I'm afraid some glass has slipped under the partition onto your side. I don't want you to cut your feet."

I stood up and stepped over to look.

"Don't step over there! Didn't you hear what I just said? There might be glass on your deck."

"Well, I don't see any."

"Would you please put some shoes on! I'm calling housekeeping," he said and disappeared back into his room.

I went inside, slipped on my flip-flops and went back outside to the couch. Within a few minutes my neighbor accompanied by a young man from housekeeping came through my room and onto my deck. "I think it slipped under here. Could you get a wet rag and wipe the area, just to make sure. I don't want these people to get cut," my neighbor said.

"There's no these people. It's just me and I really don't think any glass slipped under the partition. But thank you for your concern;

that is very thoughtful of you." I wanted them out of my room so I could enjoy our departure from Florida.

He stopped looking for glass and looked at me, squinting his eyes as if trying to figure me out. "Are you sure?"

"I'm sure. I'll wear shoes!"

"Okay, I'm sorry I bothered you. But please be careful."

I followed them to the door, then decided to watch the remainder of our departure from the running track. As I ran, I watched Florida get farther and farther away and couldn't believe I was on a cruise headed to Nassau, Bahamas. Being on the big ship was more wonderful and mysterious and romantic than I had imagined. My more spiritual clients had tried to explain it to me, but now I understood. The huge ocean was magical.

By the time I showered and headed to the buffet, no land could be seen. I dished up one of my favorite meals of spaghetti and meatballs and thought about Danielle. I wondered how she was. I found a small table by the windows, and watched the ocean as I ate my dinner. I saw my neighbor at the buffet but I ignored him.

Before heading back to my room, I couldn't help myself from looking for my neighbor to see if anybody had joined him. He was sitting alone at a table close to the buffet. *Maybe he is alone.* I wondered what his story was. It seemed a little odd to be alone on a cruise. I thought I was the only one crazy enough to travel alone.

Back outside and leaning up against the railing, I still couldn't believe I was on a cruise. I couldn't stop smiling. I was happy doing exactly what I wanted—traveling. Seeing the deep ocean from the water was completely different than seeing the ocean from a beach. It wasn't forbidding, but it was larger and more powerful than I had expected. The massive waves demanded respect, underscoring the fact that this ship and every ship was at the mercy of Mother Nature. The sun was going down quickly and it would be dark soon. I was anxious to experience my first night on the ocean.

I was tired after the hour-long water-show so I skipped the bar and drink and went back to my room to sit on my deck. In my room was a bottle of wine in a bucket with a card from my bosses at Streamline Travel. Smiling, I pulled the cork out and poured a glass, slipped on my flip-flops and stepped outside. A note taped to the partition flapped in the breeze with the message, *Sorry about the commotion earlier. Grant (your neighbor).*

I smiled mischievously, no longer feeling like drinking alone. I eased my way to the edge of the partition and peeked onto his deck. He was sitting there in shorts, loafers and no shirt. His body took my breath away. I tried to duck back out of sight to regain my composure, but he had already seen me. "Oh, hi there," he said.

"I'm sorry. I saw the note and... I, well... I have a bottle of wine and wondered if you wanted to join me." *Oh, God, that sounded so stupid.* "I see you're busy," I said, trying to backtrack.

"No, I'm not busy. I'm just catching up on some reading." He stood up. "Did you want to come over here or should I come over there?"

I smiled. "Well, the wine's over here."

"I'll be right there," he said and went into his room.

I hoped he'd leave his shirt off. Becoming excited, I realized I hadn't been with a man for over a year. I opened the door to let him in. *Damn it! He put on a shirt.* "My boss sent me a bottle of wine as a gift."

"Nice boss."

"Yeah, I'm lucky." I got another glass from the cupboard, checked to make sure it was clean and handed it to him. He held it, watching me as I poured his wine. There was something very sensual about that moment while the stream of wine filled his glass. I tilted the bottle back up and looked into his green eyes. He didn't look away and neither did I. I bit my lower lip and narrowed my eyes. My heart was thudding in my chest.

He took the bottle from me and set it on the table. "The deck?"

"Yes," I said but had a hard time moving from where I was standing. I took a deep breath and followed him.

"I'm glad to see you're wearing shoes," he said.

I sat next to him on the couch and felt like I had nothing to say but managed, "Do I know you? Have we met before?"

"I don't think so."

"It's weird. I'm sorry, you just seem really familiar. I'm sure it's nothing."

"So tell me what made you take this trip?"

"Oh, I'm trying to take a trip every year. I like to travel. How about you?"

"Well, I needed a break from work, a change of scenery."

Both of our answers were vague and I liked it. "So are you getting off in Nassau?"

"Well, yes, but I have no plans. Do you have the list of excursions?"

I went inside to get the agenda. "We get in at nine, and leave at five," I said as I sat back down next to him and our knees touched. *Oh My God. I need to take a cold shower!* "Are you single? I mean, why are you alone... on a cruise?" *Did I just ask that out loud?*

"That's a good question and one I might ask you, too."

"Is that a question? Are you asking me the same question I just asked you?"

He turned toward me and grinned. "Yes, I'm single. I don't have time for a relationship."

"You're warning me right now to stay away from you."

"Yes, I am," he said seriously, nodding his head.

"Hmm." I studied him, stared at him. He was so handsome that I couldn't stop smiling. "You've never met anybody like me before."

"I've never met anybody like anybody before."

I nodded my head and studied him some more. That was a very good point. *If I have another fling while on vacation, it wouldn't be a rebound. So what would it be and is there a chance I'll get hurt? I don't think I'll get hurt. Am I a vacation whore?* I drank the rest of my wine and stood up to get some more.

He followed me. "Are you single?"

"Yes, but I don't have a warning line other than, I'm forty-two, I don't have kids and I don't want kids." *How do you like me now?*

"Hmm." He looked at me like he was a little intrigued, but mainly unaffected. "I don't want kids either."

Taken aback, I ignored him and I reached for the bottle but he beat me to it. This time he filled my glass and it was just as sensual and exciting. Then I took the bottle from him and refilled his glass.

Again, we locked eyes. I set the bottle down and leaned in to kiss him.

He pulled back and smiled. "I warned you." He put his hand on my shoulder, pulled me to him and kissed me.

While we were upstairs making out on the bed, I understood what I was doing. I wanted flings on vacation. I wanted the safety of knowing I'd never see these men again. Grant would be another John—a vacation fling. I didn't want to get to know Grant or any other man. My life was good and I didn't need to complicate things. I didn't need the trouble of a relationship. I was resigned to being alone, but I did deserve to have fun on vacation.

While Grant was trying to take off my pants, I had to stop him. "I'm sorry. I don't have protection."

"Oh," he sighed and rolled off me.

"It's not my fault," I sat up slightly and rested on my elbows. "I didn't know my neighbor on a cruise ship would be such a pest." I giggled. "Do you have protection in your room?"

"No!" he snapped. "I didn't know my cruise ship neighbor would be so beautiful and single."

I closed my eyes and smiled. I already liked him. "Do you think there might be a gift shop or drug store on the Boardwalk or in Central Park?"

"Before we go check, let's just clear our heads." He sighed. "Let's back off a little."

I bit my lip and smiled before heading downstairs. I took a couple sips of wine, brushed my hair with my hands and said, "I'm ready."

"Okay, ah..." He glanced around my room. "Did I leave my room key on your deck?"

"I'll go check," I said, stepping outside looking around. When I looked inside through the glass door, I saw Grant fumbling with the card from my boss. I stepped inside. "No, it isn't out there."

"Okay, Amanda. Oh, um..." he said, patting his shorts, then his t-shirt pocket. "Oh, it's right here, Amanda."

I burst out laughing and bent over holding my stomach, saying, "You almost had sex... with somebody... and you didn't even know... her name."

"Alright, very funny."

"Your overuse of Amanda gave you away." I said, still laughing. "I'm sorry I didn't introduce myself."

Grant sighed loudly, walked toward the door and waited for me stop laughing. "Are you ready?"

"Yes, Grant. I'm ready, Grant." I laughed some more as we walked down the hall. I grabbed his hand and we waited for the elevator. I suddenly remembered that I vowed on my forty-second birthday to take the stairs whenever I could. "I'm going to take the stairs, I'll race you. Are we going to Central Park on the eighth floor?"

"Yes, eighth floor." The elevator bell chimed and I knew he would win but I still gave it a shot. We met by the doors going into Central Park and held hands again. We'd forgotten about the urgency we'd felt only minutes earlier, and checked out the restaurants' menus, sat on benches and admired the beauty of the ship. We watched the birds in the trees, the people on the deck and posed for a photographer to take our picture. Holding hands, we investigated the ship and made our way to the solarium and then to the very front part of the ship. There were large padded lounge chairs made for two, so we snuggled in; it was very romantic and we kissed a little and cuddled. He was well built and his body was hard. Something we had in common, we both took care of our health. I had taken better care of myself in the last year than I had my entire life. It was something I enjoyed very much.

"Do you want to do something together in Nassau?" he asked.

"Yes, I'd love to," I said and smiled.

"How about dinner tomorrow night?"

"That sounds nice."

"What about tonight?" he asked.

"Well, if we find…"

"Or we can wait," he interrupted.

"That's fine, too." After lying next to him in the lounge, I was ready to search for a drugstore, but I snuggled into his thick chest and let him hold me.

We didn't look for protection. We went back to my room, sat on the deck and finished the wine while we talked and watched people surfing in the wave pools. We were both getting tired so he walked me upstairs to my bedroom before saying goodnight and leaving.

I slept well and woke early. I pulled on shorts, my sports bra and t-shirt and went straight to the running track. It was a beautiful morning and I was looking forward to meeting up with Grant for the Nassau excursion. I figured we still had a couple hours before we pulled into Nassau, so I went to the gym area to lift some weights and saw Grant lying on one of the benches doing flies. I stepped over to him and said, "Any regrets?"

He dropped the weights, smiled and sat up. "We didn't do anything."

"Exactly," I said and stepped over to the squat rack to do a few warm-up reps before I added twenty-fives on each side. He watched. When I finished a couple sets of squats I found the hack squat, leg curl and leg press to finish off my workout for the day. I didn't look at Grant because I didn't want to be distracted, but before I left, I waved to him. I went for a quick oatmeal and hardboiled egg breakfast at the buffet.

Before I went back to my room, I found a little coffee bar and got a raspberry mocha. I showered, packed a small bag and was ready to go at nine sharp when I heard a knock at the door. Grant looked great and smelled fresh like soap. He took my hand as we walked to the elevators, then he looked at me, grinned and we took the stairs instead.

We had decided to go to the Atlantis Hotel and Casino. It sounded like the building and grounds were beautiful and I was excited to see it. I was surprised when we arrived at the casino and Grant checked us into a room. He said he got a cheap room for the day so we could use the pool and water slides and just have a place to put our things. "Oh, that's a great idea. I'll pay my half."

"Oh, don't worry about it. I'll get this one."

We were escorted to our room and Grant tipped the guy at the door. We walked inside and I immediately knew it wasn't a cheap room. In the bedroom, there was a bottle of champagne on ice next to a beautiful bouquet of flowers and an assortment of condoms lying next to the bed. Speechless, I turned and looked at Grant. He was unbuttoning his shirt and walking toward me. I dropped my bag and a rush of excitement flooded over me. I had never had a more sexy moment in my life. Grant popped the champagne, and filled our glasses. I took a few sips before Grant took my glass from me. My heart was racing. His shirt was off and he started unbuttoning my blouse while lightly rubbing against my breasts. Dropping my top onto the floor, he slipped his hand just inside my waistband as he unbuttoned and unzipped my shorts.

I swallowed hard and tried to catch my breath. I wanted to touch him but I didn't. Grant pulled the clip from my hair and let it fall against my back. He led me to the bed and pressed against me as we lay back. He gently unhooked my bra and slid it off each shoulder. He kissed my thighs as he pulled my panties down. He pulled off his own pants, reached for a condom, and slipped it on. He held my breasts and buried his face against my neck as he penetrated me.

When we finished, we rested in each other's arms and said nothing.

I broke the silence and said, "Thank you… for doing this."

"Thank you, Amanda. You are a breath of fresh air."

After another moment of silence, I asked, "Should we go swimming or check this place out?"

"Let's go investigate and if we have time we'll go for a swim."

We quickly rinsed off in the shower before putting our clothes back on and heading out to tour the place. Holding hands we walked by a beautiful sculpture and fountain of flying fish, pools of sharks and stingrays and swimming pools and water slides before making our way to the beach. We checked out the casino and shops, and split a piece of key lime pie at a restaurant near the hotel lobby that was surrounded by a huge aquarium filled with every colorful tropical fish imaginable.

On our way back to the hotel room, we opted to skip the pool and made love again. Then we collected our things, including the condoms, and called a cab to take us back to the ship. On the cab ride back, Grant asked, "If our rooms are adjoining, do you think we should open the doors separating us?"

"No. I like it the way it is. Don't you like it the way it is?"

"You're right, I do like it the way it is," he said, giving me a little squeeze.

When we got back to my room, I was happy to see our rooms were not adjoining. Grant left to see the concierge to make reservations at the steak house for seven o'clock, and I opted for a nap and a wake-up call at six.

Dinner was wonderful and the company was intriguing. Grant was special. He was polite and self-disciplined like he had a proper upbringing or maybe it was his education or he was just more mature; whatever the reason, I liked it. And because I was more comfortable in my own skin and I had a better direction in my life, Grant was just my type.

After dinner we walked along the boardwalk, rode on the carousel because I insisted, and went to a cupcake shop for a little something sweet—all the while holding hands like we were a couple just like everybody else on the cruise.

Grant was getting tired so we went back to our separate rooms. I started to get ready for bed but because I'd had a nap, the thought of going to the dance club did cross my mind. There was a knock at my door, so I ran down the stairs to see who it was and there stood Grant holding a book, wearing glasses, pajama bottoms and no shirt. "Can I stay with you tonight?"

Not sure I wanted him to, I stepped aside and let him in. "Scared? Over there all by yourself?"

"Missed you."

I smiled. He followed me up the stairs and we crawled into bed. I turned on the TV while he opened his book and began to read. I flipped through the few channels looking for something to watch. I stopped on something about jewelry in St. Thomas, our next stop, and thought about what piece of jewelry I'd get for this trip. I'd never taken off my heart since the day I bought it, and I wondered if it was time for a change. Still leaning toward a necklace, I watched TV and learned about the jewelry stores of St. Thomas and the discounts the ship's passengers could get.

"Oh, about St. Thomas, I'm not crazy about the island and thought I might stay on the ship," Grant said.

"Oh, okay. I better check out the list of excursions, or maybe I'll just do some shopping. I started this jewelry thing on my vacation to the Cayman Islands," I said, holding out my necklace for him to see. "I want to buy a piece of jewelry every time a take trip to remember it by. But the piece has to be special."

"Sentimental are we?"

"Yeah, I guess so." I was kind of glad to get St. Thomas to myself. I had heard others say it wasn't their favorite island either and I was anxious to find out why. But we still had another full day of cruising before we reached our next stop.

"Oh, and while I was with the concierge earlier today, I set up a couple's massage for us tomorrow. I hope that's okay."

"Sure, that sounds nice." I turned and looked at him. His shoulders were broad and muscular; he didn't have much hair on his defined chest but he did have that love trail of dark hair that went from his firm stomach down beneath his pajama bottoms. "Why are you single, again?"

"I don't have time."

"That's an excuse."

"You're right, I don't want a girlfriend."

I looked at him, narrowed my eyes, then smiled. "Sure seems like you do," I said in a singsong tone.

"I like my space. I like to be alone."

"I – don't – think – sooo." I gave him a questioning look.

He smiled, setting his book down on the nightstand. "I get the feeling you want to talk."

"Ah, not really," I said and looked over his body.

He smiled. "Do you know how old I am?"

"Around my age, I'd say, forty-four."

"Fifty-one."

"You are not!" I giggled.

"What's funny?"

"You don't look fifty-one," I said. "I'm just a little surprised; I thought you were closer to my age."

"Am I too old for you?" he asked.

Age has never mattered to me but it seemed he was asking as if we were headed for a relationship. I didn't know what to say. "It's just a week right?" I asked.

"You started this."

"No, I think you started it when you broke the bottle and pretended some glass slipped onto my deck."

He chuckled. "Or did you start it when you invited me over for wine and then enticed me into your bedroom?"

"That's funny… because it's true." I smiled. "I've heard that women hit their sexual prime right around my age, so let's stop with the small talk."

He slowly reached over to his book and strategically opened the pages toward the back and pulled out a condom. "Take your pajamas off and lie down."

I started laughing. "That is not romantic at all." I took the condom from him and set it on my nightstand, turned off the TV and dimmed the lights. We started making out. His body was rock solid and I couldn't get enough of his skilled touch.

While Grant was sleeping, I slipped out of bed and stepped out onto the deck. The night was amazing. Grant was amazing and fifty-one years old. He had the best sense of humor—subtle, but confident—only a secure man had that confidence. I'd never met a sexier man. I was already dreading our goodbyes because I really liked him. But I had to get over it. He had warned me and we both knew this was a one-week fling. *I'm not going to attempt a long-distance relationship. I'm not even going to give him my phone number when the cruise is over.*

The ship's lights and music turned down for the night. I walked over to the railing and looked up—I saw the most beautiful starry sky I had ever seen. It was so dark outside, like we were in the middle of a mysterious vacancy and it gave me an eerie feeling. I thought about the people who had fallen overboard over the years. I couldn't imagine what that would feel like if you survived the fall and were left floating as the ship disappeared into the blackness.

I looked up again at the twinkling night sky, wishing Grant were with me to see the stars. I moved closer to the partition to Grant's room and peeked around. His deck looked like nobody was staying in the room, with nothing left outside and everything in its place. That fit because he seemed to be a neat, organized man. I liked that about him.

I decided to go back in and try to go to sleep, but before I made it to the door, excruciating pain shot through my foot. "Oh, my God!" I yelled. I knew exactly what had happened—I had stepped on some glass. I lifted my foot to take a look and blood was everywhere. I felt faint and I didn't know what to do. I didn't want to get blood on the carpet and I didn't know if I could make my way to the bathroom. I moaned while opening the sliding door, then hollered, "Grant!"

Grant appeared like a superhero, saw me on the deck and yelled, "Sit down! I'll be right back." He propped the door open, dashed out and reappeared within seconds with medical supplies: alcohol, gauze and tweezers. He grabbed a towel from the bar area and stepped outside.

He shook his head in disbelief. "No shoes," he said as he wiped away the blood with gauze. "We need to go inside so I can see. The glass is still in your foot. Can you make it inside?"

"Yes," I said even though I felt like I might black out at any moment. There was so much blood so quickly.

He helped me inside and I sat down on a chair. I crossed my legs so I could rest my foot on my knee. He used the towel to catch the dripping blood and he wiped my cut with gauze again before pulling the glass out with the tweezers, immediately applying pressure to stop the bleeding. I watched his face and eyes as he cared for me. He grabbed some alcohol pads to clean up the small cut. "You'll be fine."

"You're a doctor, aren't you?"

He didn't answer me, just nodded. He opened a bandage, checked to make sure I was no longer bleeding, then placed the Band-Aid snuggly against my cut. "We'll get this cleaned up tomorrow," he said as he glanced out at the blood on the deck. "Let's go back to bed."

He helped me up the stairs and held onto me as we drifted to sleep. My night was restless. He was a different kind of protector than Sam had tried to be. And each time I woke with Grant's strong arms wrapped around me, I felt safe. It felt right.

God, I didn't want to go down the path of liking him and getting hurt. I had been warned, but how could I help myself. *Okay, Okay.* I breathed deeply and started focusing on getting back to my normal life in Rochester. Working hard, receiving updates from my sponsored family, going out with Sara to help her find a man, who still hadn't been lucky in love, getting ready for Teresa's wedding, and hanging out with my brother who was very lucky in sex but not so lucky in love either. Maybe I inherited the same gene as him. I wondered where I'd want to go next for my vacation. Maybe Paris and I could hook up with some French man, oui, oui. *That's better. Focus!* I liked my life, as it was—very simple.

I drifted back to sleep, dreaming of Paris and the Eiffel Tower while Grant's warm breath tickled my neck.

Chapter 20

WHEN I WOKE up the next morning, Grant was gone. I hurried out of bed, put on my running clothes and headed to the track. Skipping the gym, I ran extra laps around the track. Surprisingly, I could hardly tell that I had cut my foot the night before.

After my run I walked toward the front of the ship for a healthy breakfast at the solarium restaurant. I stepped out onto the forward deck and let the breeze and salty humidity invigorate my skin. Still amazed by the beauty and mystery of the ocean, I watched the shifting deep blue waves and thought I saw a bird, then excitedly realized that the bird was really a flying fish. Thrilled, I turned to tell somebody, but there was nobody around to tell. I looked back at the water and watched the flying fish put on their show for me.

I hurried back to the room to find out what time our massage was, and I found a note under my door. *Amanda, I'll meet you in the spa at noon. Grant.* It was only nine-thirty so I took the stairs down to the sixth floor to the rock wall. I slipped into the special rock-climbing shoes, then the harness and a helmet. The guy locked me in with a metal clasp and quickly explained how to climb and what to do when I was ready to quit. *I'm not going to quit!*

One step at a time, I made my way to the top. I rang the bell as loudly as I could. But thinking it should ring louder, I kept ringing it until two women on a deck, not far from the wall sensed my excitement and started cheering me on, so much so that I embarrassingly thanked them before I kicking myself away from the wall, gently descending straight to the padded floor. "Good job," the guy said as he unhooked me from the safety cable.

I walked away proud of myself for doing it. I had always wanted to climb a rock wall, but felt too embarrassed to try. *I'm conquering my fears. Now if only I could conquer my fear of meaningful relationships.* I wanted to shower before the massage so I went back to my room and stepped out onto the deck. Housekeeping had cleaned up the blood from my cut foot. I felt bad, because I meant to clean it up myself. I didn't want somebody else to have to clean up my mess. To my surprise, Grant was playing basketball with a few other guys. I was happy to see that he was on the skins team. *Fifty-one... hard to believe.* When the game broke up, Grant grabbed a towel, wiped his face and picked up his shirt. He glanced up at the deck. I smiled and waved. Smiling, he seemed pleased to see me watching him.

On my way to the spa, I decided to browse in the shops and look for this trip's necklace. If I found something spectacular on the ship, I could spend the few hours we had in St. Thomas exploring the island. But nothing interested me in the shops, so I headed to the spa. Grant was already in the waiting area wearing the same white robe as me. "How's your day?" I asked.

"I had a rough night, but today has been nice," he said, grinning.

"You had a rough night? I had some strange man in my bed pawing at me all night."

"Sure I was," he said and smiled. "I wasn't pawing at you; you've worn me out."

"I saw you playing basketball, you're not worn out."

An attendant stepped up to us and said, "Grant and Amanda? We're ready for you. Please follow us." We followed the young man and woman into a private room with two massage tables. "You can hang your robes here," she said, pointing to two decorative hooks on the wall, "and slip under the sheet face down. We'll be right back."

Grant removed his robe and I had to catch my breath. When he turned to hang up his robe, his ass was firm and round. He was so incredibly sexy, with his manhood hanging from a mound of dark, curly hair. "Wow," I whispered, not meaning to say it out loud.

He smiled and said, "Your turn."

I removed the robe, but still had my panties on, then quickly slid under the covers.

"Not fair."

"You've seen it."

"Not from a distance. You'll have to show me later."

The massage therapists came back into the room, my therapist, the man, asked if he should be aware of any sore spots, cuts or bruises.

"I have a cut on my foot. It's covered with a Band-Aid. It doesn't hurt."

I heard Grant chuckle, then I relaxed into the massage and fell asleep.

When the massages were over and the therapists left the room, we both took our time getting up. "Your turn."

"My turn for what?" I said and yawned.

"I want to look at your body. I want you to let me look at you."

"Fine." We both sat up and I got off the table. "Do you want me to get the lights?"

"No, I can see you."

Thank God the lights are dim. I turned around slowly and then grabbed both robes and tossed his to him.

"You have a beautiful body. You take good care of yourself, Amanda, very well proportioned and a nice shape."

"Thanks, Grant. I love working out and taking care of myself," I said and put my robe on. I loved knowing what I liked and hearing myself say it out loud.

"How's your foot?" he asked as we stepped out into the hall.

"It's fine. It's great actually. I ran a couple miles this morning and did some rock climbing with no trouble."

"I didn't see you in the gym."

"I skipped the weights today, just did cardio," I said. "And thanks for the massage."

"You're welcome," he said and grabbed my hand.

We ended up at Johnny Rockets where I ordered a grilled cheese sandwich, French fries and a vanilla shake. He seemed a little surprised, but then doubled the order. This time I bought. Johnny Rockets wasn't part of the all inclusive. Grant had been paying for everything so it was nice to give back a little.

"Do you want to get personal at all?" he asked.

And my stomach dropped. "I don't know," I said, shaking my head. "I mean you already warned me that you didn't want a girlfriend, and I have my doubts about long-distance relationships. I think you're amazing, but I'm afraid to complicate things."

"You've already complicated things," he said. "Do you have any siblings?"

"Two big brothers."

"I can see that," he said, nodding his head. "I have one little sister who lives in New York."

I was so afraid he was going to suck me in and break my heart. I wanted my gut to tell me that this was bad, but nothing was happening. I wasn't feeling anything negative or threatening. "You wouldn't believe the stars last night. They were incredibly bright and beautiful. And it was so black outside as if we were in a big black hole, very mysterious. You can only really see the stars late at night, after the ship lights have dimmed." Then I remembered. "Have you ever seen flying fish?"

"Sure, on the Discovery Channel."

"I saw them this morning when I went to the front of the ship by the Solarium."

After lunch, we stopped at the coffee bar for a raspberry-flavored espresso before our search for the flying fish. I stood next to the railing and he wrapped his arms around me from behind. I wanted to step on the railing and yell, "I'm the king of the world," like Leonardo DiCaprio in the movie *Titanic*, but I decided against it. We quietly watched and waited. "You'll think you're seeing a dark silver bird, but it's really a flying fish," I said.

After about fifteen minutes he said, "Maybe morning is the better time to see them."

"Maybe," I said, disappointed, "or maybe it was the area we were in this morning." I turned and he stepped in front of me, pressing me against the railing. He kissed me softly and I gently bit his bottom lip. He kissed me harder. I bit him again and he put his hand up through my hair at the back of my head and pulled slowly as he continued kissing me. I felt weak and out of breath. My heart was pounding.

Looking into my eyes, he said, "What if I told you I was falling in love with you?"

I said nothing. *Please don't hurt me. Please don't hurt me.* I tried to lighten the moment, saying, "You warned me."

"We have enough in common, Amanda. We both workout and take good care of ourselves. We don't want kids. We are independent enough to travel alone. We like to get up early. We both want to travel. We get each other's sense of humor. We fit well together and I can see you in my life."

I turned back to face the water, but he stayed close to me, pressing his groin against my hip. He slipped his hands up my shirt and caressed my breasts. "Should we go to my room?"

He held my hand and led me to his room. "Maybe you'll lose some of your power if you're in my room," he teased.

We made love and, for the first time in my life, I sensed something real was happening—as if love was being exchanged.

An hour later, Grant ordered room service while I snooped through his closet. "Can I wear this shirt tomorrow?" I asked, stepping away from the closet and holding it up for him to see.

"No, it wouldn't fit you."

"No, I know. I'd wear it like a dress with a belt. Oh, I don't have a belt," I said and hung it back up. "Can I look in your suitcase?"

"Sure, but I think it's empty. I have stuff in the bathroom you can go through."

"Oh, that's a good idea," I agreed and walked into his bathroom. I looked at his toothbrush, smelled his cologne and brushed my hair with his brush. When I finished, I jumped onto the bed. "What did you order me?"

"You didn't just use my brush, did you?"

"Yes," I said and smiled. But the smile quickly faded and tears welled up in my eyes. "I'm scared."

"Of what, Amanda."

"Falling for you."

He smiled, and said, "That's more like it."

Unable to help myself, I sank deeper into this romance I did not want. Desperately looking around, I said, "I know, hit me!"

He looked up over his glasses. "I don't have the energy," he said.

"Um… Call me a bitch or better yet a cunt."

"You cunt," he said dryly.

"Ugh! Don't sound sexy when you say it! Well, this isn't working."

There was a knock at the door and Grant got up to get our food. "Come with me and help." He started down the stairs. "Tomorrow night is formal night and I think we should go. I can rent a tux."

"Can I rent a dress?"

"I don't think so. You don't have a formal dress?"

"No."

"Well, we'll have to get you one."

We ate our delicious meal in bed—salmon with rice and broccoli and large glasses of skim milk. When we finished, I said, "Maybe we should go dancing," as I started downstairs with the trays to set on the table by the mini bar.

"I'm afraid you're on your own. I don't dance."

"Well, you'll at least go for a walk with me, right?" I yelled up to him.

"Sure." He came downstairs with another tray. "I have to go and get measured for the tux; the shop's by that flower stand."

On our way, we checked out the smoky casino, bought some of the pictures that the ship's photographers had taken of us, and found our way back to the cupcake shop. "Are you still staying on board tomorrow in St. Thomas?"

"I've been thinking about that, and maybe I will join you for a little while. I think we have five or six hours," he said and took a bite of his half of the cupcake. "Do you have plans? Did you book an excursion?"

"No, I thought maybe I'd look for a necklace and well now, a formal dress. And if I have time I'd like to grab a cab and take a mini tour of the island's hotspots."

"That sounds like a busy day."

"What would *you* like to do in St. Thomas?"

"Follow you around," he said and reached across the table to hold my hand. "Ready for bed?"

"Yes, I'm exhausted."

"Sure you are," he said and grinned.

We held hands and started toward the stairs. "Have you seen the running track?"

"No, I haven't, in fact."

"Would you like to? It's just one floor down."

"I'd love to," he said following me down the stairs and outside.

Night on the ocean was mysterious and called to me. When I was outside in the breeze, I was more drawn to the dark sea and sky than I was to Grant. I stepped off the track and next to the railing to look into the blackness. I glanced up at the sky full of stars. "Maybe I'll see you here tomorrow morning before we disembark." I turned around to face Grant and rested against the railing.

He jumped up and down on the track a little. "This is nice. There's a little give."

"The best part for me is being outside with the view."

We made our way back to his room and I was grateful because I had every intention of sneaking out once he fell asleep. I was looking forward to the night and bed to myself, especially considering he'd decided to join me in St. Thomas. I needed a little space to sort out my feelings.

About an hour after tucking ourselves in, Grant was fast asleep and I eased my way out of bed and out of his room. When I opened my door and stepped into my room, relief flooded over me, then just as suddenly unexpected loneliness. If I'd had his room key, I might have gone back. Instead, I went out on the deck with a bottle of Perrier. I lay down on the couch and looked up into the clear, black sky filled with millions of stars sparkling brilliantly.

I was lost in the deep vastness of the twinkling sky thinking about how I wanted to open myself up for love. Grant was giving me a taste of what might be possible and I wondered if there was any way that we could continue our new romance after the cruise. I sat in silence and looked to the stars. *I wish Grant would stop saying the things that make me wonder if he truly wants more. He's confusing me.* I wanted to stay open to Grant but detached enough so I wouldn't get hurt. *If I can walk the fine line, and this turns out to be nothing more than a cruise-ship fling, I will be okay. I have to stay detached.*

If this doesn't go any further with Grant, maybe I'd open myself up to possible future relationships when I get back to Rochester. Maybe I'd join Sara in the search for love. Maybe we should try some speed dating or online dating together. Who knows, maybe there is somebody who would be a perfect fit for me. Rochester was growing and I was pretty sure I hadn't met everybody yet. Maybe it should be my new goal. *Maybe I will invest a little money into finding a suitable mate, instead of saving money to continue on these vacation flings.* I was ready to put my vacation-whore days behind me. I didn't want to take another trip alone. I wanted to have fun with somebody who I knew, not a stranger.

I thanked the stars for making things clearer for me and decided if Grant was not meant to be, there were plenty of stars in the sky. I sat up, took another drink of water and slowly made my way to bed. I fell asleep as soon as my head hit the pillow.

The next morning I went straight to the running track, feeling well rested and excited about St. Thomas. After about three laps somebody was running right behind me and wouldn't pass. I was getting irritated. *I'm sorry I'm not a fast runner.* I slowed down to a walk hoping they'd pass me, then I remembered it was probably Grant, so I turned around and there he was with a big smile on his face.

"Good morning," he said, stepping next to me. "You didn't want to sleep with me?"

"I'm sorry, I…"

"It's okay. It's new for me, too. How was your night?"

"My night was amazing. The stars were beautiful and I've made myself a promise to be open to possibilities."

"That's great news. I'll send a moving van for you when we get back so you can move in with me."

I smiled but said nothing. *That's the stuff I want him to stop saying.*

"We only have an hour before we can disembark. I'm done with my workout. Thanks for showing me the track. It's a beautiful morning and great to be outside. Where should we meet? And what about breakfast?"

"I guess I got a later start than I wanted, so I'll go for a run later. Should we head to the buffet and grab something? I'd kill for a raspberry mocha."

"Are you sure?"

"Yeah, I'll grab a workout before our formal night. What if I can't find a dress?"

"I think we'll find one…"

"Okay, wait a minute," I said, stopping him. "I've never gone shopping for clothes with a man before, other than my brothers, and I'm very nervous about this."

"Painless," he said and smiled. "Everything is under control."

Chapter 21

AS WE LEFT the ship, we had our picture taken like we were a
real couple—Amanda and Grant in St. Thomas. Holding hands, we
rushed to the shopping area and went to the first jewelry store we
saw. I told Grant to sit down on a bench just outside the store so I
could look by myself. I told him it was very important to me and I
had to look alone; the necklace had to be perfect and I wasn't sure
what I wanted but I knew I didn't want his influence. Just like I had
done in the Cayman Islands, I started at one side of the store and
looked at everything. About half-way through, with only one possibility, I heard, "Amanda?"

I looked up and saw John. "Oh, my God! How are you? What
are you doing here?"

"What are you doing here? You look great!"

"Thanks, so do you. Oh, I'm on that big ship, Oasis…"

"Let me guess, you're looking for a necklace?"

"Yes!" I reached up and showed him my heart. "I've never taken
it off."

"God, I've missed you," he said and reached across the counter
for my hand.

I let my hand slip away from his. "John, I'm sorry, I'm with someone." I pointed toward the door and saw that Grant was now inside the store browsing himself.

"I blew it. I let you get away. How long have you been together?"

"It doesn't matter, John. Long distance doesn't work; it's too hard."

He rubbed his fingers through his hair, then locked them behind his head and sighed. He looked up for a moment, then said, "Alright, let's get you that necklace."

"You were important to me, John. I won't forget you."

He smiled. "Follow me. What are you thinking?"

"What do you have with black stones?"

"Well, we have black coral. Here, take a look at these." He pulled out a small black star.

"That's it, that's the one I want. But just the pendant; I want to keep the chain I have. I love this chain; it's the perfect length and thickness."

He looked up at me and grinned as if I were talking about his penis.

"You know what I mean," I said and smiled.

"Well, you are quick about this, just as decisive as the last time," he said as Grant walked up next to me.

"Did you find something you like?"

"Yes," I said and pointed as John held it up.

"It's beautiful. I'd like to buy it for you," Grant said.

"No, Grant, thank you. I have to take care of this myself, it's important to me."

He looked at John. "I tried."

John smiled and told me to take off my chain so he could clean it and make sure the pendant slips as it should. I unhooked the clasp and set the chain on the counter, then turned to Grant and said,

"John helped me with this necklace about a year ago in the Cayman Islands."

"Wow, small world."

"I know, that's what I was thinking."

"Has it been a year?" John asked.

"Yes, almost exactly a year."

"Would you like me to box up your heart?" John asked.

I smiled. "Yes, I guess it's time to box up my heart and move on to something new."

I left the store with my new black star around my neck—I absolutely loved it. The black was for the dark sky and ocean at night and the star was for the beautiful starry nights.

Grant grabbed my hand and we ran across the street to Gucci. "I saw this place while you were looking at the jewelry."

"Grant, I can't afford Gucci."

"Come on, I think they have some good deals."

We stepped inside and a woman walked toward us, "Grant, right? I'm Cindy."

"This is Amanda."

She reached out and shook my hand. "You guessed her size right; she's a four," she said to Grant. "Let me show you what we have."

I gave Grant a look. "You lined this up? Grant, I really can't afford this."

"Shhh," he hushed me. "I got this one."

Not about to let him buy me a Gucci dress, I started calculating the expense of this trip and how much I would be willing to spend on a dress. I had originally thought I would find a dress for two hundred dollars or so, not in the thousands. I started manipulating numbers trying to justify spending at the most fifteen hundred. I wasn't a designer person, so this would probably be the only piece I'd ever own. And why not own a beautiful Gucci dress that I could have for years?

The first dress I saw, I wanted: It was a black strapless gown with a slight gather at the waist. It was simple but elegant and perfect for me. I hoped it would fit and look good on me. I casually tried to find the price—three grand. *Not a chance.* I assumed the simplest dress would be the least expensive so I felt defeated. "Grant, come on, let's go. I don't even want to try them on. They're beautiful, but way out of my price range."

"I told you, I got this one. I'm the one who wanted to go to formal night," he said. "Listen, I don't have a wife or a girlfriend to spend money on. Let me do this for you." He was sincere.

"Are you sure?"

"I'm sure." He turned and looked at the four dresses. "Do you like the red one or this white one?"

"If you're buying, you're choosing," I said. Oh, how I hoped that wasn't a mistake.

"Fair enough, I need to see you in all of them."

"I figured you did," I said and smiled as I walked toward the dressing room with Cindy following me carrying the dresses.

I tried on the black one first and I loved it, and if he didn't pick it, I considered buying it myself. I stepped out of the dressing room and he immediately scrunched up his face and said, "Next."

My heart fell. *He doesn't know anything about beautiful dresses. Great, he'll probably pick the one I like the least.* I tried on the red one next and then the tan one, which made me look naked. I put on the white one last and felt like I was getting married. I loved the dress, but I just didn't want a white one. He seemed to like every dress but the black one. I put my clothes back on and came out of the dressing room. Cindy was handing Grant back his credit card. "You bought one?"

"Yes."

"Which one?"

Grant just smiled at me and turned to Cindy, saying, "Wrap it up so she won't know which one I chose for her. And we'll pick it up in a couple of hours."

Cindy smiled and said, "They were all beautiful on her."

"Cindy, tell me which one," I begged. "Sisterhood, Cindy, sisterhood," I pleaded. "Give me a hint."

"I can't. I'm sorry."

I turned to Grant and said, "I'll get you back."

He raised his eyebrows and smiled. "Let's get a cab and check out this island."

When we got back to the ship, I was happy. I loved my new necklace and I'd had a great day with Grant. We'd gone to a lookout point to admire the different islands and the magnificence of the vast ocean. Seeing this island and its sister islands from such height was spectacular. And the best part was my companion—there was nobody I'd have rather seen it with than Grant. Every moment I spent with him made me see what an incredible man he was. He was so kind and so wonderful I didn't think there was a woman alive good enough for him.

I went for a quick run as the ship was leaving St. Thomas. Then, I rushed back to join Grant on his deck and watched St. Thomas fade into the horizon. It was time to get ready for the formal dinner, so I went back to my room. I opened the closet door and stood there speechless—the black Gucci dress hung there, even more beautiful than I remembered. I started laughing and dancing around the room in the joy of having the most beautiful dress and the most beautiful man in the world.

I showered, put on a little more makeup than normal. I defused my hair and wore it up with curls hanging loosely around my face—I wanted to look beautiful for Grant. I wanted him to be proud to have me walking next to him. When I heard the knock, I took a deep breath and glided over to the door. I opened it and forgot all about my dress, my hair, me. In front of me stood the most stunning man I had ever seen. He took my breath away. I stood there with my mouth open, trying to speak but couldn't. I couldn't believe this gorgeous dark-haired, green-eyed man was my date for the night. "You look amazing," I said and suddenly felt small and insignificant and not good enough.

"And you are striking. That dress was made for you, and I knew it the second I saw it."

"Thank you so much. I've never had anything so beautiful."

"Neither have I."

"You're going to make me cry."

He kissed me, tenderly on the lips then on my chin. "Let's hurry with dinner so I can get that dress off of you. I think it would look better on the floor."

We made our way to the formal dining area and didn't take our time eating. He might have had plans to get me into bed, but I had plans to get him on the dance floor. He had kept the dress a secret, so I'd keep my dancing plans a secret.

When we got into the elevator, I pushed a button and quickly turned to kiss him so he wouldn't see where we were headed. But he didn't seem to notice until we stepped off the elevator and he asked, "Where are we?"

"We're going to dance."

"Oh, Amanda, I don't dance."

"Three songs, that's it."

"You know what? Let's do it. I don't know anybody but you, and you can't hold it against me because you're forcing me."

"That's right, I am. I want you to dance with me."

"Lead the way."

Grant started off trying to slow dance with me to a fast-paced, hip-hop song. The second song he seemed to feel the rhythm, and by the third song, he was just having fun and now I was the one wanting to get him into bed. I was ready to dance between the sheets.

We made our way to Central Park to get our picture taken all dressed up. The photographer said we were the best-looking couple he'd shot all night. I knew he said that to everybody, but I did believe that Grant was the best-looking man he'd taken all night.

When we walked through a lounge to get a glass of wine, heads turned to stare as we passed. Grant slowed us down, it seemed, so they could get a good look. I was definitely proud to have him next to me and maybe he was proud to have me on his arm, too. I felt like the luckiest woman alive, envied by all the other women on the ship.

When we got back to my room, he took off his jacket and we went straight upstairs. He turned me around, unzipped my dress and let it drop to the floor. I turned toward him wearing nothing but black panties and black pumps. I unbuttoned his cuffs, unhooked his tie then started unbuttoning his shirt. I slid my hands against his firm chest and pushed his shirt over his shoulders and let it drop to the floor. I unzipped his pants and let my hands ride his waist to his tight ass. I slid my hands into his boxers and slid them down his hard thighs as I kneeled down and kissed his inner thigh. I made my way up to his balls and breathed in the scent of him. I slowly licked the hair on his stomach going up to his chest. He buried his face in my neck and we found the bed. He lay me back and we made love for what seemed like hours. We slept through the night and woke in each other's arms in the morning.

We skipped the morning workout, figuring our sexual workout had been enough, and went for breakfast before getting off the ship in St. Maarten. In a cab, we toured the half-French, half-Dutch island. I loved our cab driver, a huge overweight man who sweated profusely and huffed and puffed every time he got in and out of the cab. His sport jacket cut into his arms every time he honked and waved at his many friends on the island. He was a cheerful man who told us that he lived between two of the best restaurants on the island and that was why he was such a big man. Driving through the shopping area, he commented on the wonderful perfume shops. "I love perfume," he said. "In fact, I wear perfume. I'm a big man and perfume smells better and lasts longer than any men's cologne I've ever tried." He wiped his head with a hanky. "I'm not embarrassed. My friends think I should be embarrassed, but I'm not. I love women's perfume."

On our way back to the ship, we were stuck in a traffic jam because of road construction. I started to panic. Would the ship leave us? How long would they wait? Suddenly our cab driver wasn't so charming after all. I was angry at him, thinking he had to have known about the construction. I remembered the *island time* mentality of islanders from my Cayman Island trip. I should have remembered and planned for it.

Seeing my nervousness, Grant pulled me back against the seat and told me to relax. "It's fine. We'll make it in time."

"How do you know? How can you be so sure?"

The cab driver overheard and said, "No problem. I'll have you there in time. We're only about fifteen minutes away."

I took a deep breath and tried to relax. Grant wrapped his arm around me and pulled me close. "There are some nice hotels here; we'll be fine either way. If the boat leaves without us, we'll have a fun adventure."

Oh my God! You're not helping! I don't want an adventure like that! I want to get to the ship on time! I smiled politely even though I was completely stressed out. I sat up again to watch the road and traffic, and I heard Grant laugh a little.

"This is a new and very interesting side to Amanda," he said just as the view of the ship came into sight.

"Oh, thank God," I said as Grant and the cab driver continued their teasing.

We made it back on the ship with plenty of time to spare, and I was finally able to relax.

Chapter 22

WHEN WE GOT back to his room, we agreed that a nap was in order. Grant spooned me and wrapped his arms around me, making me feel safe and loved and protected. Suddenly and unexpectedly, I was happy that every other man had walked away from me, that every other man decided I wasn't good enough.

After a few hours of deep sleep, we wandered around the ship looking for something to eat—we were both starving. We settled on Johnny Rockets for grilled cheese again. At the table next to us, people were talking about a couple who did not make it back on the ship on time. "Did you hear that?" I whispered to Grant.

"Yep."

I felt like I was going to have a panic attack. "How could that happen?" I demanded.

"Probably having too much fun at a local bar and lost track of time."

"Or there was that time change, remember? What if they thought they still had an hour… Oh, my God," I said and took a quick gulp of my shake.

"Maybe they were in a car accident and they're in the hospital."

"Oh, don't say that."

"Maybe they went to the beach and a shark got 'em," he said, grinning.

"That's not funny."

"Or maybe they were murdered by a local serial killer."

Ugh. I gave him a dirty look.

"Amanda, they were probably having fun in a bar and lost track of time. They'll catch up with us in Fort Lauderdale."

I gave him a questioning look. "That could have been us."

"But it wasn't. Amanda, you're adventurous. You took this cruise by yourself, so why does this bother you so much?"

"I'm not sure," I said, but it was probably because I was a travel agent and a little more sensitive about the passengers. I wouldn't want a cruise ship leaving any of my clients.

There may have been even deeper issues at work. St. Maarten was the last stop on our cruise. Our stops were over and now it was a straight shot back to Ft. Lauderdale and then back to Minnesota and then back to my life without Grant. We had one day at sea and the next morning our trip would be over. I tried not to think about it, but sadness overwhelmed me every time I remembered that my time with Grant was coming to an end. My heart was hurting.

Sipping wine, we sat on my deck moving deeper into the night. We were both quiet. "Well, this is where it all began," I said and tried to smile.

"Not for me."

"What do you mean?"

"I noticed you during the safety demonstration. You gave your chair to an older woman and then found a chair for her husband," he said and reached for my hand. "You seemed like a nice person… and strong, those chairs weren't light." He grinned. "Then I saw you right next to me in the hall. I couldn't imagine you were alone, but I hoped you were."

I smiled thinking about that first night. "Did you break the glass on purpose?" I asked, hoping that he did.

"You'll never know," he said with a devious smile.

I closed my eyes and smiled. Grant was the closest thing to love I'd felt in a long time. Grant was no Nick, Sam or even John who were more interested in their wants and needs than mine. Grant genuinely seemed to want to learn about me. But this time, I wasn't opening up or trying to learn about Grant. I felt like I was making a terrible mistake, but I didn't know how to protect myself while staying open to possibilities. "You're the greatest guy I've ever known, well, besides my dad and brothers, and I hate that this is coming to an end." I stood up, walked to the railing then turned around to look at him. "One more day. Oh, and when we get back to Ft. Lauderdale, I'm going to do that early checkout, you know, where we can take our own bags off. I have a morning flight."

"I'm doing the early checkout, too. Are you flying out of Ft. Lauderdale or Miami?" he asked.

"Lauderdale."

"Me too. I guess we could share a cab."

"Sure," I said with a lump in my throat. "But," I paused, "we still have the rest of tonight and all day tomorrow. And I don't know about you, but I haven't gotten enough sun, so I was thinking of spending the day at the pool. I found out that the people in these lofts get a special lounging area, a little more private."

"I'm going to figure you out," he said. "But right now, I can't put my finger on how you can afford one of these lofts, but yet you are very money conscious with everything else?"

"Well, I can't afford it really, but I got lucky and I save my money like a stingy person all year so I can take nice vacations to reward my hard work."

"Last year was the Cayman Islands?"

"That's right, and I'm thinking Paris next year."

"I'll go with you."

I smiled and looked down. "That would be nice. That would be very nice." Just then, the music shut off from the ship's sound system and the lights dimmed. "Oh, my God," I said excitedly and reached for my star necklace then I grabbed Grant's hands to help him up. "This is when you can see the stars so clearly." We leaned against the railing and he draped his arms around me and held me as we looked up at the star-filled, black sky in silence. A tear trickled down my cheek.

We didn't make love that night or the next morning. Everything was winding down, we had an early morning workout, breakfast, a quick coffee stop, then to the pool to search out our special lounge area. We drank whatever drink special they had and I had a little too much. I tried hard to act normal but Grant kept laughing at me and I realized there was no hiding the fact that I was buzzed, maybe even drunk. I called the server over and asked him to please bring me the biggest bottle of water they had and some food. Something with bread. "Come here," I said pulling the server closer to me. "I think I had too much to drink, and I don't want to make a fool of myself in front of my boyfriend. It's our last day together."

The server laughed and walked away.

I turned to Grant. "Please help me. I don't want to feel like this on our last day together. What should I do?"

"Time, it will take some time. And just so there is no confusion, I'm buzzed too. Those drinks were strong."

"Oh, thank God." I felt a little better knowing Grant was under the influence, too. "I think I've had enough sun. I'm ready to go if you are." I told the guy to cancel my order and we went straight up to my room. I hadn't felt so buzzed or drunk since I was in the Cayman Islands with Steve. I didn't like feeling out of control.

I was glad that I'd kept my head together because Grant didn't, and before he entered me he claimed he wanted to feel me and mumbled something about making a baby. *Oh, my God!* If that doesn't sober a person up quickly! If I hadn't been so aroused, I would have laughed. I made him wear a condom.

Maybe we both got drunk to cover up our feelings of sadness because our time together was coming to an end. After some wild, fun, drunken sex, we got dressed and went to the buffet to eat.

Still a little buzzed but feeling much better, I convinced him that we needed to go ice skating. So we made our way down to the fourth floor, put on our skates and slipped on the mandatory helmets. I took off first and I was very shaky remembering my rollerskating wipe-out. I stayed close to the railing. Grant, on the other hand, knew how to skate. I was shocked and somewhat embarrassed because I had thought I would be the better skater. But after about three laps around the small rink, I considered myself an Olympic figure skater. I tried to do the triple, spin and skate around on one leg with my other leg gracefully lifted behind me and my arms spread out wide. I felt fearless and young and I knew I'd try to rollerskate again once I was back home. Grant's tricks were more of a hockey player's maneuvers, going as fast as he could, then stopping on a dime. I landed on my rear over and over again, but he never fell.

Chapter 23

I DIDN'T SLEEP at all that night and, even though I was in his room and I could have left, I didn't. I stayed with him all night, our last night, not wanting the night to end, wanting to stay wrapped in his arms forever. For one week we were in love, and I didn't want to lose his love. I was so afraid of the day, so afraid I wasn't going to be strong enough to say goodbye.

About twenty minutes before our five am wake-up call, I started to cry. We would share a cab and say our good-byes, and then I would go back to my life in Rochester and Grant would go back to his life. If we did exchange phone numbers, which neither he nor I had suggested, we would eventually lose track of each other. Why prolong the inevitable. I thought a clean break is better—I'll try to stay strong.

I rolled over and faced him. I put my hand against his cheek and he opened his eyes. "I don't want it to end," he whispered.

"Neither do I."

"Do you want to try?"

"I do, but..."

"This isn't over… It can't be over."

My heart was thudding and I didn't know what to say. "You told me you didn't want a girlfriend. You warned me," I said, trying to smile.

"I know." He put his hand on my cheek, and felt my tears. "I don't want to hurt you, Amanda."

"Too late." I swallowed hard and tears flooded my eyes. "I had a wonderful time, better than I ever could have had alone."

"Me too."

"I'll never forget you."

"I hope not."

"I'm sorry," I said softly.

"For what?"

"I wish I was better at this."

He smiled, saying, "You're perfect."

The tears poured down from my eyes and my whole body was crying out to tell him that I loved him. But I couldn't say the words. "Thank you. I think you're perfect, too."

The phone rang and he rolled over to pick it up and set it back down. "Are you all packed?"

"Yeah, just about."

"I'm going to order a little something to eat. So come over here after you shower."

"Okay." I thought about going to my room, skipping the shower, packing up and getting out of there just to avoid the inevitable. I wanted to get it over with. It didn't sound like he believed we had a chance and he had warned me. Teddy had always told me it's a man's actions, not his words, that count because guys will say anything in the moment to get their needs or wants met. And maybe Grant's wants were to avoid hurting me and a smooth separation.

I made my way back to my room telling myself, *I'll be okay. I'm ready to get back home. I have a Paris trip to look forward to.*

I quickly showered and got dressed. I skipped the mascara; I was prepared for future tears.

Grant let me in and we quickly ate some oatmeal and fruit. I was thankful he'd ordered coffee. We didn't talk. After we finished breakfast, I went back in my room to get my suitcase. We were all about the business of getting off the ship as efficiently as possible. Once we were in the cab, the small talk began and some fishing began. I knew what this was, the dance of separation. "So do you have a lot of work when you get back?"

"Probably. How about you?" I asked.

"Oh, yeah, I'll be busy. I'll bet your family, your brothers missed you."

"Yeah." This was painful, so I decided to lighten the moment. "You wanted to make a baby with me last night."

He burst out laughing and wrapped his arm around me, holding me tightly. "Oh, Amanda."

Once he paid for the cab and we collected our luggage, we said our goodbyes. I stayed strong. I knew this was over and I was fine. I'd had an amazing time, better than the Caymans. I cried a few tears and we had a long hug that neither of us wanted to break. As I walked away, he called my name, "Amanda."

I turned around to see if he was going to stop me and tell me he loved me and ask for my phone number.

"I'm joining you in Paris," he shouted.

I smiled and kept walking while fighting the tears. I wanted to believe it wasn't over. I turned around to get one last glance at Grant. I saw him make a gesture to two young men in Army uniforms. The guys made the same gesture back and smiled. I shook my head in disbelief that I could let the most spectacular man I had ever met, walk away from me.

I checked in for the flight, grabbed a raspberry mocha from Starbucks and went straight to my gate. I decided I'd allow myself the rest of the day to cry, but then I had to snap out of it. And not only was my heart aching from losing Grant, but my body was starting to ache from my ridiculous ice-skating exhibition the day before.

The ticket agent was just getting ready to open the gate for boarding so I stepped up to be first in line. Even though I wasn't first class, she looked at my tears and sadness, gave me an understanding smile and allowed me to board. She probably thought I qualified as needing extra time. I found my window seat toward the back of the plane, threw my purse on the floor in front of me and closed the blind. Grabbing the blanket that was on the seat next to mine, I buckled myself in and covered up. Digging out some chapstick in my purse, I saw the box that held my heart. I opened it and saw a folded-up piece of paper. *Amanda, please call me if things don't work out with Grant. I've really missed you and I'd like to give us a try. I was such a fool. John 972-555-5754.*

I'm a vacation whore. What is wrong with me? I finished off my raspberry mocha, stuck the cup in my seat pocket and the heart and John's note back in my purse. I closed my eyes and snuggled in hoping to sleep all the way home.

I woke about thirty minutes before landing when I heard the captain talk about the recent snowstorm in Minnesota. Besides the turbulence during descent, it had been a perfect flight with the time going quickly.

After we landed, I pulled myself together, reapplied chapstick, picked up my purse and slipped back into my shoes. I got off the plane and started walking through the crowd to baggage claim. A man stepped out of the men's room carrying a coat, a man who looked like Grant from behind. He was on his cellphone. *I'm sure everybody's going to look like Grant for a while.* I kept walking and looking at him; he even walked like Grant. I walked faster to catch up to him, and there he was. "Grant!"

He turned around and stopped. "Wow," he said, stunned. "Were we on the same flight?"

"I guess."

He seemed rushed, nervous and distant. "I have to catch my next flight. I'm sorry," he said.

"Oh, of course, yeah, I gotta go, too."

He turned around and hurried away from me.

I'm such a fucking idiot! I turned and walked back the other way completely devastated. How could I have thought there was something more between us? That was our last conversation. That was what I had to remember him by, "I have to catch my flight. I'm sorry." *Are you kidding me? I have to catch my flight. I'm sorry.* I liked "I'm joining you in Paris" much better. I dropped my purse on the floor and sat down against the wall and started crying. All the times I felt small and insignificant next to him, I was. God! What did I get myself into? *I have to catch my flight. I'm sorry.* I hung my head between my legs and kept crying.

One of the flight attendants from the flight I had been on, stopped next to me and stood at my feet. "He's not worth it. Don't want a man who doesn't want you back. Don't waste those tears on a man who doesn't care. The right man will never allow you to feel like this. He'll move mountains to make sure you never feel the way you feel right now."

Don't want a man who doesn't want you back. "You're right." I had tricked myself into believing this was different, he was different.

She helped me up and put her arm around me. "You'll be fine."

"You're right. Thank you." I said and tried to smile. *I'll be fine. I'll be fine.*

I found my suitcase sitting next to the conveyor. Baggage from another flight was already coming in. I wheeled my suitcase through the snow out to the shuttle for a ride to my car. It was freezing outside. After brushing off the snow and scrapping the windows, I had to sit in my car for twenty minutes to warm it up. While I waited, I opened the glove box and a photo of Sam dropped out onto the passenger seat. The Al Green CD was sitting there, so I stuck it in the player and listened, turning the vents toward my icy hands gripping the steering wheel. *I have to catch my flight. I'm sorry. I have to catch my flight. I'm sorry.*

Chapter 24

THE NEXT WEEK I tried to get back to my normal life. I threw myself into work and tried to move past the "I have to catch my flight," shocker. I tried to pretend that the last thing he said to me was that he wanted to go to Paris together. But I thought the sting of "I have to catch my flight" was just the reality check I needed.

I got my usual update about Sam from his friend. Sam was doing fine but still mentioned me often while talking to his friends. "Sam said that he acted like a fool and he wished he hadn't walked away from you," his friend told me. I just shook my head and wished Grant felt that way.

"When are you going to go out with me?" his friend asked.

"I'm not."

"Sounds like you might be a good catch."

"I'm not," I said, and told him to stop calling me. "I don't want to know about Sam anymore, but if you see him or talk to him, tell him I wish him well."

"I'm not going to tell him I talk to you. He'd kill me if he knew I was calling you."

"But still, you need to stop calling and I need to put all of this behind me."

He said he understood and we said good-bye. As much as I liked the updates and the occasional flirting, everything before Grant seemed so foreign and distant. I had changed and I didn't want to be pulled back into the past.

So that weekend I spent boxing up everything in my apartment that reminded me of Nick or Sam or John or Grant. I stuck all of it in my closet—the stuffed dog from Danielle went into the box, the Al Green CD went in the box, and photos of Sam and photos of Grant and me from the cruise went into the box. I kept my Gucci dress covered with a garment bag in the back of my closet and placed my heart in a small, red jewelry box that I rarely opened. I thought about not wearing my star for a while but decided it was my gift to myself and I wanted to gain strength from the star. But the black of the coral now matched the dark emptiness I felt inside, and as much as I tried, I couldn't see a star in the cloudy, cold, Minnesota sky.

After boxing up my memories, I felt like I needed to vent, tell somebody the truth, so I called my brother, who was just on his way home from work. He made a detour to my door.

"Now what's going on?"

"Oh, God. Where do I start?"

"Start with Sam. Is Sam still bugging you?"

"No, it's a combination. I don't know what I'm doing wrong." I said blotting my eyes as if there'd be tears. "You know about the Cayman trip I planned for us... and then he dumped me for the second time, remember?" I exhaled. "Well on that trip, I met a man, John."

Teddy started laughing, "I didn't know that. This story is already more interesting. Continue."

"It's not funny; it's complicated."

"I'm here to help," he said trying to sound serious.

"So I had this nice three-day fling with John, who worked with jewelry and was there on business. We went out for dinner three nights in a row and he helped me get over Sam. John called a few times after I got back, but it was never a good fit; he wanted children."

"Got it."

"Well," I said, "so that whole experience I think was very good for me. Sam tried to get back with me after I returned and well, because I had been with somebody else, I couldn't go back, you know, that's how I am. I knew it was over with Sam or I wouldn't have been with John. John was good for me.

"I got ya, you had a good healthy rebound. So what's the problem?"

"Well, after that, I didn't drink. I didn't date anyone, or go out much. I didn't really do anything, you know?"

"Yes, boring. I know."

"Not boring, as much as trying to figure out my life. I was also focused on saving money and taking another trip—I like traveling. Hence, the Oasis. So, on the ship, I met somebody and we quickly, well, it had been a year for me, you know." I took a deep breath and ignored Teddy's smothered laughter. "I was on vacation, maybe a little lonely. Everybody was in pairs, except for me and, well, Grant. So we hooked up, and I initially decided I was a vacation whore and I was okay with that."

Teddy interrupted, laughing, "What? Wait a minute. A vacation whore?"

I started laughing, too. "This isn't funny. I have a sick, sick problem and I need help."

He looked up and rubbed his chin like he was thinking. "Another meaningless fling while on vacation... I think it's brilliant!" He reached over to high-five me. "Man, women are lucky! I'd never be so lucky on a cruise. I mean, maybe I could hook up with somebody from the ship's kitchen staff who barely speaks English...Was it staff? Let me guess, a twenty-one year old bartender on the ship."

"Oh," I sighed deeply, "I wish. No, Grant was perfect and I think I fell in love with him," I said, "He warned me that he didn't want a girlfriend. But I fell for him anyway."

"Well, I guess you're not a vacation whore after all."

"I really meant to be. I wish I was, but he was just so amazing. We had some things in common... he didn't want kids," I said trying to convince him.

"Well, are you going to try the long-distance thing?"

"No. It's done. He didn't feel the same way about me."

"How do you know?"

"Well, the last words he said to me were, "I have to catch my flight, I'm sorry," and he rushed off. He was trying to get away from me at the airport. The fantasy was over."

"Ouch. Is he married?"

"I really don't think so. God, I hope not. I thought he was one of those bachelor guys, you know, never been married, didn't want kids."

"Amanda, your choice in men is bizarre! Sam? And then this guy, who tells you he doesn't want a girlfriend but you go for it anyway. Come on, Amanda!"

"You don't know, Teddy. Our time together was incredible." I looked down. "Grant felt right to me. It just seemed like we were on the same page all the time, until the end, but you know, it wasn't his fault. We agreed that we'd have this whirlwind romance on the ship and that it would be over when the ship docked. I just didn't know I'd feel this way."

"You fear commitment, Amanda. You purposely pick the wrong guys. What are you afraid of?"

I felt like I had a light-bulb moment. "I don't want what I had with Nick."

"SO STOP PICKING GUYS LIKE NICK!"

I started crying and stared at Teddy. It seemed so simple. I was picking guys like Nick—unavailable men who were not interested in me. "You just gave me a breakthrough."

"You're welcome."

I wiped my eyes, then my nose. "Can I try to give you a breakthrough?"

He smiled and said, "I don't need one anymore. I have a girlfriend."

"You do not!"

"I do. And I like her a lot."

"Wow! Who is she? How did you meet?"

"The old fashioned way—at a bar."

"Oops!"

"Oh, that's coming from the original vacation whore."

I sighed.

"Amanda, you picked a self-described bachelor on a week-long vacation. Mandy, you gotta pick better." He lifted his eyebrows and looked me in the eyes. "I'm sorry. It was one small week of your huge life. You'll get over it. Stop crying and pick a better guy next time... or don't. You don't have to be with anyone."

"Grant kept saying things to make me think he really cared about me."

"Oh, Amanda. I told you, you can't listen to a man's words—actions only."

"I thought his actions looked pretty good, too." I took a deep breath and shook my head. "You're right, you're right. I'll mourn him tonight and be done with it." I stood up and hugged Teddy. "Thanks for coming over... My next trip is Paris. I'm going to find a nice French man," I said and tried to laugh.

Teddy laughed and broke our hug. "Well, at least you're thinking about the future... and you can laugh."

"Thanks for letting me vent." I walked him to the door. "When do I get to meet your girlfriend?"

"She's special. We're going to take our time."

I started crying again and put my hand on my heart. "Thanks Teddy. You give me hope. Your girlfriend's very lucky."

"Amanda. Look, you've been on this quest to find yourself and you've done it. You know who you are and what you want and you're staying true to that. You take good care of yourself. You want to travel and you're doing that. You've made peace with yourself about not having kids. You're good to people, you care about your clients. For God sakes, you give money every month to somebody you've never met. You're a good catch and if you're sad right now, it's your own fault." He grabbed me and gave me another hug. "Grow up, Mandy, You're fuck'n forty-two. You deserve a good guy if you truly want one and you deserve to be happy."

I loved his tough love and when the laugher beat out the tears, he left and I locked the door behind him. Within five minutes, there was a knock on the door and, figuring he'd left his keys, I glanced over the room before I opened the door to tell him I didn't see them, but when I opened the door it wasn't Teddy. It was Sam.

He stepped into the apartment and closed the door behind him. "I want to talk. I want to be with you. I can't get over you no matter how hard I try or who I date," he said in a rush. "I just can't get over you."

Just the sight of him made me weak. Even though time had passed and we'd both moved on, there was some fire and passion still there—so dangerous, so unhealthy, so tempting.

I looked at him, studying him, remembering everything. I took him by the hand and led him to the couch. I sat next to him, holding on to him and I cried. He cried, too. He tried to kiss me. He tried to take me to the bedroom. But I simply shook my head no. I loved the way he smelled, I would never forget his scent. And how big and protective he seemed. I buried my face in his chest smelling his leather jacket mix with his cologne and cigarette smoke. He held onto me and comforted me for the first time, but I wasn't crying for him. I was crying for Grant.

He wiped the tears from my face and brushed my hair back. "Why didn't we make it work?" he asked.

"I don't know. Timing maybe."

"I won't hurt you anymore."

"I know." *Because I won't let you.*

"It can't be over, Amanda."

"Sam, we were never a good fit. I thought I could force you into what I wanted, but you had different wants and needs. I'm sorry I didn't see that earlier," I said and wiped my eyes.

"Amanda, you were always so distant. I couldn't get in, I couldn't break through to you to show you how much I loved you. You didn't care to know," Sam said and then, he stuck a knife in me and twisted it with his words, "My girlfriend's pregnant."

I was dumbfounded. I gently closed my eyes in disbelief. I took in a few deep breaths. "Sam, why are you here?"

"I don't know... I...I would run away with you right now, just the two of us... I just..."

I stood up facing him and shook my head. "You have to go," I said, too upset to cry anymore. "I want you to leave and I don't want you to ever come back. Don't call me. Don't stop by my work. Don't stop by my apartment. Stay away from me." I walked over to the door and opened it.

He walked out, turned around to say something, then changed his mind. He left.

I went straight to my gym, turned the music as loud as I could without disturbing the neighbors and started running on the treadmill. I thought about Teddy's advice; he was right, but I wondered what I got out of feeling sorry for myself; what was my payoff? Did I like the sympathy? Or did I just like being right living in my self-ful-filling prophecy? Whether I wanted to admit it or not, I knew what I was doing.

Yes, Grant's last words made me sad. Especially because I thought maybe we had something special. I had been misled, I had misled myself. But I can't let a few words or the few seconds it took him to say them, destroy me. It's okay. I'm okay. I'm not going to cry over him or anybody else. My life's pretty good, I have a great family, the best friends, I love my job and my apartment. I'm healthy and I take good care of myself. I'm financially secure. I get to help and watch a young family grow. I have fond memories with men who simply were not right for me.

After almost an hour on the treadmill, I wiped my face with my small towel and went into the bathroom for a quick shower. I missed Grant, not enough to cry about any more, but I missed him. *Oh, this sucks!* I stepped out of the shower and dried off before getting into my pajamas.

I got under the covers, rolled over and snuggled a pillow. I thought about Grant and hoped he was happy, and I hoped he thought about me. And although it wasn't meant to be for us, he was the closest I'd come to my ideal life partner, which gave me hope. I was building momentum and I was getting closer to what I wanted. The best was yet to come.

Chapter 25

I'D BEEN BACK in Rochester for a couple of weeks and I was finally starting to get on a roll with work and giving men very little thought. Then Friday afternoon I heard a familiar voice and peeked out from behind my office door.

I almost passed out. Grant was standing at Sara's desk wearing a suit and holding flowers. "I meant to get these for you last week, but I was busy with work," he said, setting the bouquet next to her computer, then sitting down at her desk.

Sara smelled the flowers and thanked him. "They're beautiful."

My heart was in my stomach and I was paralyzed, but I continued to listen.

"I just wanted to thank you for the most amazing trip of my life," Grant said.

"I'm glad you had a nice time. How was the room?"

"It was great. Say, before I forget, you don't have access to the list of passengers from the cruise I was on, do you?" Grant didn't seem the same. He was nervous and somewhat awkward.

"No, I'm sure it's a privacy issue."

"Oh, right. Do you have any phone numbers of somebody who might be able to help me get that information?"

"I'm going to have to check with my boss."

Oh God, please don't call me… don't call me…

"Okay," he said, and gave her his card. "Could you give me a call once you check with him?"

"I have your number," Sara said quickly.

"Just a reminder." He set his card down in front of her.

"Sure, I'll let you know what *she* says," she said and picked up his card.

"Oh, I mean she. Okay then. Thank you. Thank you again for arranging such a wonderful trip." He pushed his chair in and left the office.

I couldn't get my mind around what had just happened. So I stayed in back until Sara and the others left for the day. I turned the light off in my office and closed the door. I stepped next to Sara's desk to read the card on the flowers from Grant. *Sara, Thank you for your help. I had a wonderful time. Dr. Dillard.*

I sat down at her desk, searched and found Grant's business card—he was a Mayo doctor and lived in good old Rochester, Minnesota. I couldn't believe it. It had to be a dream. As I turned to get up from Sara's desk, I hit my leg on her drawer. "Ouch!" I said, holding my knee. *Okay so it's not a dream.* So the flight he was rushing to was a Minneapolis to Rochester flight, a twenty minute trip by plane. I drove the hour and a half drive in the snow and he flew.

I just couldn't believe what I was learning about Grant and I couldn't believe he was suddenly back in my life, sort of. Still in shock, I went home for another exhausting run on the treadmill to try to clear my mind. I needed to burn off my nervous energy. I needed to let this sink in—the most amazing man I've ever met, and possibly the great love of my life, lives in Rochester, Minnesota.

I didn't sleep at all that night, and I nervously cried every moment I was awake. I was in a state of denial. The thought of Grant living in Minnesota had never crossed my mind, much less in Rochester. The odds of that were preposterous. I wanted to, yet dreaded running into him; it was much easier thinking all I had to do was get over him. I couldn't decide if Grant living in Rochester was a bad thing or a good thing. My mind kept racing with every possible scenario of what might happen next.

Sara had been acting differently since I got back, and then she got flowers from Grant. Was there something going on between them? Sara was beautiful and any man would be lucky to have her. "Oh, I hate my life," I said, rolling over and burying my head in the pillow.

And what would I say if I ran into him? *Maybe I'd ignore him and pretend like I didn't know him.* After all, that's how he treated me at the Minneapolis airport, like he didn't even know me, like we hadn't spent the most wonderful week of our lives together, well, the most wonderful week of *my* life. *Oh, God, what am I going to do?*

Around seven the next morning, I was happy to head out of town. It was Rob's birthday and we were having a family get together. My parents and I were spending the night with Rob but Teddy couldn't because of work, and I assumed he didn't want to be away from his new girlfriend. We stayed so busy with the kids and visiting with each other that I had very few thoughts of Grant. It was a wonderful weekend. Whenever I spent time with my family, I realized how much I missed them.

Unfortunately, I couldn't find the same distractions at work on Monday. Sara came into my office and sat down. She was flipping a business card against her chin. "Amanda, some strange guy, well, one of my clients wants to get the names and phone numbers of everybody that was on the cruise he was on. That isn't possible, right?"

Suddenly, I heard what she was asking me—what he had asked her—and my heart missed a beat. *Was it even possible that he would try to find me? Is that what he was asking for?* "I don't think that's possible, but I guess you could give him the number of the cruise line." I took a sip of my mocha. "That's a strange request. Did he tell you why?"

"No, not really. He said he'd had the time of his life. Maybe he wants to buy everyone a bottle of wine or something." She stood up to leave. "Hey, you were on the same ship! You went on the Oasis, right? I guess I could give him your name and number; maybe you'll get a free bottle of wine." She laughed. "Did anything exciting happen on the ship that would make a person want everybody's name and number?"

"I don't think so, but what do I know? It was my first cruise. I would assume it was a typical cruise, lots of rest and relaxation."

"Really? Rest and relaxation, huh?" She scoffed sarcastically and left my office.

Now what the hell was that all about? I followed her and watched as she sat down at her desk and dialed Grant's number. "Hi, Dr. Dillard. This is Sara from Streamline Travel. I spoke with my boss and we don't have access to that information, but let me give you the phone number to the cruise line… Maybe somebody there can help you get a register of the ship's passengers. Good luck and I'm looking forward to helping you with your future vacation plans," she said and threw his business card in the garbage can.

Well, even if he liked her, she didn't like him. That was good news, and maybe he was trying to get in touch with me. Maybe that's what this was about; maybe he really did have a great time. Maybe… Then I heard his words again. *I have to catch my flight. I'm sorry. I have to catch my flight. I'm sorry.* I lowered my head onto my desk and sighed.

Again, I waited for everybody to leave the office before I closed up. I went through Sara's garbage and dug out Grant's business card. I held it to my nose to try to catch a faint scent of him.

Instead of going home I went straight to Teddy's. There was no answer but the door wasn't locked, so I walked in figuring he'd be right back. I thought I heard something in his bedroom so I slowly opened the door, "Teddy?"

"Wait," he yelled.

But before he could say, "Don't come in!" I had pushed his door open and was face-to-face with Teddy's ass and Sara's shocked expression.

Teddy grabbed the covers and rolled off Sara.

I stepped out, closed the door and yelled from the hallway. "Oh, my God. Sara! I knew something was up!"

When they joined me in the living room, I looked at Teddy and pointed at Sara. "Teddy! This is the girl?" Then I looked back at Sara. "Sara, I warned you about him. What are you thinking?"

"Amanda! What do you mean you warned her about me?" Teddy demanded.

"Amanda! I'm a grown woman. I wanted this... I needed to have some fun." Sara finally spoke.

"Oh, God, Sara! That's how it starts..."

"I don't think a vacation whore should be giving me advice."

"Oh!" I snapped at Teddy. "You told her?"

"Hey, what can I say? She's my girlfriend."

"Really?" I said dramatically, putting my hand over my heart. "Neither of you could have picked better. I adore you both. I'm so happy for you. So how long has this been going on?" I expected Sara to say two weeks.

"About three months," she said.

"You have not!"

"Yes, maybe even four."

"Why didn't you tell me?"

"I don't know. We wanted to ride it out for a while to see if we were a good fit. We haven't told a soul and we don't want you to tell anyone either. We'll tell when we're ready."

"Four months, wow! I guess I've been preoccupied." I took a deep breath. "I won't tell anybody."

"Teddy told me about your trip and some guy you fell for."

"Yeah, now I know why you laughed when I told you my trip was filled with R and R."

"I couldn't help it and I was a little pissed you didn't tell me. I thought I was your best friend."

"Sara, I'm embarrassed by my behavior; the fewer people who know, the better. My brother just happens to be a great shoulder to cry on and he's the exact opposite of judgmental."

She flashed a proud smile and nodded. "You're right, that he is."

"So I was a mess the other night; I unloaded everything on Teddy. I needed to tell somebody."

"You know I'm here for you," Sara said as she reached over and squeezed my leg. "Hey, I know you had a loft suit on the cruise ship. I checked the computer. In fact, it looks like you might have been right next to Dr. Dillard. Did you ever run into him? Do you know who he is?" She smiled. "I wasn't trying to be snoopy, but out of curiosity I checked both your rooms and well..."

My heart dropped. I didn't want Sara to know who this mystery man was or that he lived in Rochester, but because of everything Teddy told her I could see the wheels turning. I needed to figure this out before she did. "Oh, really? I..." I wanted to tell Teddy everything I had learned about Grant, but suddenly I thought maybe it was Sara I needed to talk to. "Sara, call me when Teddy goes to work," I said, giving her a quick hug before I left.

Chapter 26

AT HOME, I ran a little on the treadmill and lifted some weights. Then I called Teresa to see if I could come over for awhile, but they were just walking out the door, to go to the mall to get a few things for their wedding. She said I was welcome to join them.

"Thanks, I'll just see what's on TV or rent a movie.

"You sound pathetic."

"I am pathetic."

"Come on, come out to the mall with us. We'll go for a drink after," Teresa coaxed. "Well, call my cell if you change your mind. I have to go."

I wanted to talk to somebody. I wondered if I should call Grant. I held his business card in my hand, flicking it against my chin just as Sara had. I just wish I knew how he felt. I didn't want to put myself out there unless I was sure he would meet me half way.

The phone rang and Sara said, "I'm on my way over. Let's go get some pie."

"You're a lifesaver, Sara. I'll be waiting outside."

Sara picked me up and we drove the three blocks to the pie shop.

"So what do you know?" I asked Sara.

"I'm pretty sure I know all of it."

I was touched because I'd never known my brother to open up or share anything with a woman before, and it was nice to see that he cared about Sara. I was happy that Sara didn't listen to my warnings and she gave Teddy a chance. Grabbing her hands, I said, "I'm so glad you're with Teddy. I want to hear all about it. How did it happen?"

"Later," she said. "I want to know about your cruise. And who is this John from Cayman?"

"Did Teddy tell you that I fell in love with this man from the cruise?"

"Yes, he told me you fell in love with the George Clooney type." She grinned.

"That's cute. Well, something has come up, Sara, and now you're involved, more than you think."

The server walked up to our table, and I ordered a large glass of milk and a triple berry pie. Sara ordered a large glass of milk and the French silk pie.

"Alright, let's hear it," Sara said.

I took a deep breath. "On the cruise I fell in love with this amazing man. When we were saying our goodbyes, it felt unfinished, like we would see each other again. He kept making comments, like, 'I don't want this to end.' and 'I'm going with you to Paris next year.' Stuff like that." I took a few big gulps of milk and continued. "Then, I discovered we had been on the same plane and I saw him again at the Minneapolis airport. But this time, when I saw him, he acted cold and rushed to get away from me. All he said was, 'I have to catch my flight, I'm sorry.' Just 'I have to catch my flight, I'm sorry.'"

"Ah, that hurts."

"Yes, it felt like I'd been sucker punched; I'd never felt so stupid. Am I really that hopeless and naive?"

The server set our pie down in front of us and walked away. We both quickly lifted our plates and exchanged pies, while smiling. "Are you sure? Maybe you could use some chocolate."

I giggled and took a few bites from my berry pie with whipped cream. "Oh, I love this stuff. Anyway, what do you think so far?"

"I don't want to upset you, Amanda, but it sounds like he knew all the right things to say, and, well, he used you."

I smiled. "Okay, good. We're on the same page."

"Good?"

"There's more to this story." I broke off a piece of my crust and ate it. "Teddy helped me see that I was just a bad picker and I started feeling better, you know, getting a grip on the situation." I looked at Sara. "This is where you come into the story." I shook my head. "Gosh, how do I tell you this? You might already have an idea."

"Tell me."

"Well, like I said, I was feeling better about everything and then on Friday afternoon…" I reached into my purse and pulled out Grant's business card. I set it in front of her. "This man came into Streamline Travel."

"So. Dr. Dillard. What does that mean?" she said, and then suddenly got it. "Dr. Dillard?"

"Yes, he's the man I'm in love with. Grant Dillard."

Sara was laughing out of control. "Dr. Dillard? No way! Oh, my God!"

"I guess when he was running late for his flight, I assumed to another state, he was just flying to Rochester."

Sara kept giggling and staring at me. "He's hot." She smiled and nodded her head approvingly.

"You know what? Just sit with this for a minute. Then tell me what to do. I don't want to run into him. I don't know what to do."

Sara finished her pie, drank down the last of her milk and kept staring at me and giggling. "I just can't see it. He's older than you right?" She looked at me sideways. "I think your joking."

"Ugh. I'm not joking. Let's go. I'll show you the pictures to prove I'm not kidding. Let's pay and go." I grabbed Grant's card and stuck it back in my purse.

At my place, we went straight into the bedroom and I pulled down the box from my closet. My throat tightened and I started fighting the tears right away. I pulled the photos out of the box first. Then I took the garment cover off the dress he bought me.

Before Sara made herself comfortable on my bed, she gave me a disapproving look. "Jesus, Amanda, when are you going to get a bed? You need to get your bed up off the floor. A mattress on the floor is not good for your love life. This could be your whole problem!" She took the photo from me and stared at it for what seemed like a several minutes. "I can't believe it. He looks so different and you both look so happy." She turned the photo for me to look at. "I've never seen *you* look happier."

I took the picture from her. "I was happy." I looked at it again. "What am I going to do?"

Sara led me back to the living room and we sat down on the couch together. "What I know for sure is that he had the time of his life on that cruise. He told me so." She squeezed my hand and smiled. "I don't know for sure, but in my opinion, now that I know about you, I have to wonder if he is searching for you. Why he was so cold to you at the airport in Minneapolis, I really don't understand that."

"That's the one thing that makes me sure that he is not interested in a relationship with me. He was so distant at the Minneapolis airport."

"It's possible that he did have a great fling with you, but then when he got home he missed you. So now he's looking for you, I mean, that's possible, right?"

"I just wish I knew how he felt. I'd like to avoid any further rejection or embarrassment."

"Well, if you would allow me to investigate, I would like to help you get some answers."

But the thought of Sara finding out the truth, knowing the truth before me, seemed too painful, humiliating. I didn't want Sara to be the one to tell me Grant wasn't interested and that it was just a fling, and truthfully, I didn't want to hear that from Grant either. "I'm not sure what I want to do. But I have to ask you, why don't you like him? On Friday when he came in, I sensed that you didn't care for him."

"Oh, Amanda, it's nothing."

"Tell me, Sara." My stomach turned, fearing the worst.

"It's just that he looks like an old boss of mine who was very condescending and belonged to the old boys' club, if you know what I mean. He didn't respect women and well, Dr. Dillard kind of looks like him."

"I remember him. You had to quit your job because of that jerk."

"Yep, that's the one. So really, I have nothing against Dr. Dillard." Sara laughed. "So what are you going to do? Let's say you were just a fling to him."

"Well, I'm going to have to find a way to make him fall in love with me, of course!" I teased.

"You are a glutton for punishment."

"Yep, and I now know what I've been doing—I lost myself with Nick, I punished myself with Sam but enjoyed good sex, I learned to listen to my gut with John, and then during the time to myself, I found myself but then Grant came along to test me. I hope I don't fail this test."

"What if he misses you and he's looking for you?"

My chest tightened. "I'm scared."

"Ah, duh! You let this amazing man walk away from you. And here you sit, afraid of running into him. You have his phone number in your purse and that's as far as it goes," she said. "You need to grow a set."

"I know. I really do." I took a drink of my water. "If it hadn't been for the way he treated me at the airport, this wouldn't even be an issue."

"Okay, forget about what he's thinking or what he wants. What do you want?"

"I want Grant."

"Great!" she said and headed straight to my bedroom.

I curiously followed.

She grabbed my box with memories of past men and dug out more photos of Grant. She took the box with photos of Sam and other miscellaneous memories to the kitchen and threw it into the garbage.

I started laughing and crying at the same time. Next she went back into my bedroom and found a picture frame with a photo of my parents inside. "First of all, your parents do not belong in your bedroom." She opened the frame and let the photo drop to the floor. She reached for a picture of Grant and me from our formal night on the cruise ship and stuck it into the frame.

I kept laughing while tears flooded my eyes. I stood by and watched Sara make over my bedroom.

She set the framed picture front and center on my small nightstand by my mattress. "Wait a minute!" she said, then set the frame on my desk. "Help me!" She reached down and I helped her move my mattress to the center of the room instead of shoved up against the wall. She moved the little nightstand by the side of the bed and set the picture frame on top. "You're bed has to be in a position that two people can get in and out comfortably," she said as she looked around my bedroom. "You have to make room for love."

The symbolism of everything she was doing felt refreshing as if I was letting go of old hurts and making room for something wonderful.

"I need something red for this corner." She looked around my room and grabbed my small red jewelry box that held my heart charm that I got in Grand Cayman. She set it on the floor in the corner. "Leave this here, okay? It's important."

"Okay," I said. "How did you learn about this stuff?"

"I read it in a magazine," she said and started laughing. "That sounds so bad! But, I did it to my bedroom and three days later I hooked up with your brother." She smiled and winked at me. "My bed used to be against the wall, too. Granted, I had an actual bed. Amanda, you gotta get a bed!"

"I know."

"Tomorrow! We're going tomorrow after work. I know a guy who works at that big furniture store on 52. He'll give you a deal. I won't take no for an answer. I know you want to save your money, blah, blah, blah, but tomorrow, we're getting you a big-girl bed!"

After Sara left, I went back into the kitchen and pulled the box from the garbage. I went through each memory-attached item, starting with the note from John. *Amanda, Please call me if things don't work out with Grant. I've really missed you and I'd like to give us a try. I was such a fool. John 972-555-5754.* I tore it up and threw it into the garbage can. I cuddled the white stuffed dog Danielle had given me. I kissed it and wished Danielle well, then put the dog in the garbage. The Al Green CD went next. After studying photos of Sam and Nick, I wished them well and let them go into the garbage. The note Sam had put on my windshield, *I was thinking about you,* went into the garbage. I kept my room key from the cruise ship.

I didn't cry. I reached for my phone and dialed Sara's number knowing she was at my brother's place. "Hey, Sara, I just wanted to thank you for tonight. You're a great friend."

Chapter 27

THE NEXT NIGHT after work, Sara and I went to a furniture store to find a proper bed. I was excited because the few things she had changed in my room felt really good. I loved seeing Grant and me on my nightstand before I fell asleep and I felt hopeful. I figured a new bed couldn't hurt.

When we got to the store, Sara's friend was on crutches with a cast on his leg. "Jeff! What happened to you? Oh, my God! When did this happen? What happened? And why didn't you tell me?"

He chuckled. "Settle down, Sara. I was in a car accident along with about twenty others. You know that pileup on I-90 a couple weeks ago? I was one of the lucky ones."

"Oh, my God! You were in that wreck! Oh, my God! How many people died?"

"Well, out of the twenty some cars, only one person died. It was a miracle."

"That's right, it was an older man who died, right?"

"Yeah. Check this out." He lifted his hair up off his forehead to reveal a red scar. "I was messed up, and I've only been back to work for a couple of days."

"I heard bits and pieces about the pileup. Did that happen while I was on the cruise?" I asked Sara.

"Yeah, I think so," she said distractedly as she touched Jeff's forehead.

"Hey, my doctor had been on a cruise, too. I think he came back early or something. He saved my life. Well, my life and a few others."

Sara jerked her head my way with a startled look on her face. "Dr. Dillard!"

"Yeah, that's right. How did you know?" Jeff asked.

The room started spinning, my mind started racing and I barely heard the rest of the conversation.

"Oh, he's my client at the travel agency," Sara said.

"I love him. Isn't he great?"

"Yeah, he really is. Well, show us what you have for beds." We followed Jeff as he hopped on his crutches toward the bedroom sets and Sara excitedly squeezed on my arm. "That's why he was in a hurry at the airport!"

I tried to stop thinking about Grant so I could pay attention to Jeff, but I wanted to get out of there. I bought a modern queen-sized bed with a light wood headboard that had padded leather squares because it reminded me of the bed I'd had on the cruise ship, the bed I'd shared with Grant, and two matching night stands. I would have loved a king bed but I knew I didn't have the room. Sensing my distraction, Sara demanded a rush delivery and setup the next day.

The following day I got off work an hour early to wait for my new bed. I couldn't believe how excited I was about a bed. I couldn't wait for a new mattress and an adult bed, instead of the dorm-like mattress lying on the floor. When I got home I distracted myself by cleaning, organizing and moving my desk into the living room to make room for my new furniture. I was anxious and energized.

After the bed was delivered and set up, I went to the mall with Teresa for new bedding for me and a bridal shower gift for her. Their wedding was only a few months away in the early spring. She was the only bride I'd ever known who wanted it to snow on her wedding day because to her, there was nothing more romantic than a fresh, spring snowstorm. And Rochester was known for having some wonderful spring snowfalls.

I bought crisp white bedding with a few blue and green throw pillows—the same colors that were in the cruise ship bedroom. I bought Teresa what she wanted, a nice bottle of wine. Like she said, they both had their own places before they moved in together and they had lived together for months, all the while buying what they needed, so they registered at a liquor store. They wanted parties and get-togethers with all their family and friends and they wanted to have wine and drinks to share. They wanted their place to be a spot for friends, a place to hang for an hour or a couple days; they loved company.

When I got home I excitedly made my bed, took a hot shower then slipped naked between my new sheets. I reached for the picture frame and gave Grant a kiss goodnight.

Chapter 28

THURSDAY EVENING, TWENTY minutes before closing,
Sara and I were the only two left in the office. I heard her make a
funny noise and then, I heard, "Hi, Dr. Dillard," she said loudly so
I'd know he was there. I stayed behind my office door listening with
my heart pounding.

"Hi, Sara. Thanks for getting that phone number for me," he
said and sat down. "I've been getting the run around, but I got a hold
of somebody who can help me. He understands the situation so I
think he may find her for me. I just wanted to say thanks again, and
ah, while I'm here, could I get some information on Paris and maybe
London, I don't know, a tour maybe, I'm not sure."

"Sure, what's your timeframe?" she asked while taking notes.

"Well, not right away. I just want to get some ideas and start
planning."

"Can I ask you why you want everybody's name and number
from the Oasis cruise?"

"Well, I don't want everybody's, just one person's number. I met
an amazing woman on the ship, and I'm not sure why I let her sneak
off without getting her phone number. I guess I didn't think it would
be so hard to track her down," he said. "But I'll find her. It's just
going to take a little time and maybe some money."

"Oh," Sara said and giggled.

"What?"

"I don't know," she said and started laughing, then said, "Hey, I ran into a patient of yours, Jeff. He said he had been in that pileup on I-90 a few weeks ago. Weren't you on the cruise when we had that bad wreck?"

"I had just gotten back. In fact, Amanda, the woman from the cruise, was at the Minneapolis airport waiting to catch her next flight, but I was distracted by the accident. All the patients were headed to Saint Marys and Methodist, and they needed doctors. I was so focused on getting to Saint Marys as quickly as possible that I don't even remember what we said to each other."

"Wow, and you just walked away from her?" Sara said with a critical tone.

He lowered his head. "Yeah, it's like I had a second chance to tell her how I felt, but I blew it."

Sara chuckled, then coughed to mask her bad manners."Um, did you say her name was Amanda?"

"Yes, Amanda," he said. "Not until the patients were stable did I realize what I had done. I never should have let her get away from me."

"Oh, I have some news for you. I did find one person who was on the ship with you," she said and started laughing uncontrollably.

"Sara, are you okay?"

"My boss was on the cruise with you."

Oh, God please don't. Not right now. My heart was racing.

"Oh," he said, not understanding why that should matter.

Sara started laughing even harder. "Oh, boss, could you come out here?"

Nervously I stepped in front of a small mirror on the wall and checked my face and teeth. *Oh God.*

"Oh, boss!" Sara said even louder, still giggling.

I took a deep breath and stepped out from behind the wall. "Yes, Sara, did you need something?" I said looking in her direction, not in Grant's.

When Grant stood up, I performed my best surprised reaction. "Grant!"

Sara was quietly hiding her laughter.

He rushed passed Sara's desk and grabbed me. "Oh, my God, Amanda!" He held me tightly in his arms. "You work here?"

"Yes."

Grant laughed in disbelief. "That's amazing," he said.

Sara stood up and started gathering her things. "Well, my work is done here."

He looked at Sara, then back at me, tilting his head to the side and asked, "Okay, how long did you know?"

"I don't know, about week," I said looking at Sara.

She nodded her head in agreement. "Oh, and by the way," Sara said, "Dr. Dillard, I can't be your travel agent anymore. You're going to have to work with my boss. You'll like her, she's nice." She smiled. "I can't wait to tell your brother," she said, and left.

Grant pulled me close to him. He pressed against me even harder and gently kissed my lips. "You didn't want to talk about anything personal," he whispered. "Yes, it was fun and exciting and crazy to be so secretive, but I wasn't about to let you get away from me. Not a chance."

"I can't believe you live here." I said and buried my face against his neck.

Grant tightened his grip on me. "Are you ready for all of this?"

I grinned and said, "I'm ready."

"When do I get to meet your family?"

I smiled. "Soon."

He kissed me. "My room or yours?"

"Mine. I just got a new bed."

"I can't stay all night."

"Good, my bed's not that big."

Grant laughed and I knew that was the laugh I wanted to hear for the rest of my life. "How much trouble are you going to give me? I want you to move in with me; I want you around. I don't want to lose you again."

"And this is coming from Mr. I don't want a girlfriend, Mr. I don't have time for a relationship."

"Okay, I see you're going to give me trouble." He kissed me gently again. "That's fine, I guess I have some work to do. Come on, let's go." Grant took my bag from me as I locked the door. He continued carrying my bag and holding my hand as he walked me to my car. "I'll follow you."

"I hope so," I said, smiling.

"Do you think you should come to my place instead, so you can see where we live?"

"I can't stay all night."

He smiled, licked his lips while studying me, and said, "You might want to."

I smiled back, knowing I wouldn't because I had to work the next morning, but I wasn't going to argue with him.

"Come with me. I'll drive you back to your car when you've had enough of me."

Hardly speaking, we turned and walked arm and arm to his car, a nice BMW SUV. He opened the door for me and handed me my bag. His dark hair and handsome face reignited the fire in me. I couldn't wait to love him again. I could feel my body reacting to my excitement and I started feeling lightheaded—I couldn't believe I was with Grant again and this amazing man wanted to be with me.

We pulled into his clean and empty three-car garage, and then walked into his house. I felt a little uncomfortable. He'd lived a lot of years without me. He had a past and memories inside. If he was a bachelor, how many women had been in and out of this house? How and why would I be different or enough so he'd want to keep me around? Insecurities continued surfacing as he led me to the kitchen. "Amanda, come here." He turned on a dim light and reached for a wrapped box from inside one of his cupboards. "This is for you." He handed me the box. There was a note taped to the small package. *To: Amanda, the most beautiful woman in the world.*

I unwrapped the box and found a key inside. I gave Grant a questioning look.

"It's the key to this house." He turned. "This is for you, too." He handed me a garage-door opener. "This is for your car, for the garage." He opened the refrigerator and guided me to look. "I don't know everything about you, but I think you like Perrier, right?" Grant had an entire shelf filled with bottles of the sparkling water. He opened one and handed it to me.

"Yes, I like Perrier." I smiled and took a sip. "Thank you."

"Oh, and I have this coffee and espresso maker." He opened a drawer that was filled with raspberry-flavored coffee, syrup and pods.

I closed my eyes and fought my tears. I smiled and kissed Grant. "Thank you."

"You're not the only one who did some snooping," he said and escorted me to the master bedroom.

I noticed Grant had the same photo of us framed and on his nightstand.

"I bought a few things for you. Your shampoo and conditioner are in the shower, along with a toothbrush and Close Up toothpaste. I'm assuming you brush your teeth in the shower. I've never known anybody to do that but while you were sleeping on the ship, I noticed that your toothbrush and toothpaste were in the shower. Am I right? Do you brush your teeth in the shower?"

"Yes, you're right. I brush my teeth in the shower," I said and laughed.

He flashed a proud smile. "Your perfume and deodorant are here and I've emptied these drawers for you. Oh, and I bought you your own hairbrush." He grinned then opened a drawer. "I don't know anything about makeup really, but I saw this at the store and I remembered you had the same pink and green mascara." He held up the unopened package. "I've made space for you in the master closet, too." He led me to the closet. "I bought you one of the shirts you liked of mine and a few belts; I didn't know what kind of belt you would like to wear. Oh, and I bought you this jewelry case for your necklaces," he said and opened it to show me the empty jewelry box. "For all your necklaces when we travel."

"When did you do all of this? What if you couldn't find me?"

"I had to find you, Amanda. I had to."

I expected to make our way to the bed, but instead Grant held my hand and we went into his living room. He flipped the switch and turned on the fireplace. "Amanda," he said and turned around to face me. He took a deep breath. "Amanda, I played every scenario in my mind of how this would work, but I never dreamed that you lived here in Rochester. This changes everything. I believe the timing is right and I hope you feel the same way."

I wanted to lighten the mood, but Grant was so serious, so I decided to listen to him make his case as to why I should move in with him. My answer was already yes.

"Once the urgency of the I-90 accident was behind me, I couldn't think about anything else but you. Every trip to the grocery store, I picked up items I thought you might like. Every time I was running late, I thought of you being upset with the perfume-wearing cab driver. I rarely take the elevator anymore, and I haven't eaten so many grilled-cheese sandwiches since I was a kid." He chuckled nervously. "Every night without you in my life is torture and if I am able to sleep, my dreams are only about you." He smiled. "Amanda, I want to learn everything about you, I want to know your hopes and dreams." He took a deep breath. "I don't know how you did it, but you've taken over my heart and my mind. I knew that night when I met you on the ship that my life would never be the same. You warned me, and you were right, I've never met anybody like you."

He uneasily turned back toward the fireplace and pulled something from the black stone mantel. Then he walked over to me and knelt down on one knee.

With my heart racing, I tried to catch my breath and started to cry.

"Amanda, I'll never be the same and it's because of you," he said emotionally. "I know this is sudden, but I can't imagine my life without you. I don't want a girlfriend. I don't have time for a girlfriend. I want you to be my wife." He opened the small box to show me the ring. "Amanda, will you marry me?"

I whispered, "Yes" as I wiped my tears.

Chapter 29

I MOVED IN with Grant that weekend, but I kept my apartment until the lease was up, just for a little security and space if I needed it. I was scared to make the move, but I couldn't imagine my life without Grant. He cared about me and wanted me in his life; he proved that because every word he spoke matched his actions. And I made sure my actions and words matched my intentions, too—I wanted to spend the rest of my life loving Grant.

I found myself hurrying to play catch-up, wanting to know everything about him. I learned quickly that Grant was a bit of a workaholic, so I understood why he wanted an independent woman who didn't mind time to herself. His long hours at the hospital gave me the time and the final push to start my own travel agency. Teddy and Sara joked that I should call my business The Vacation Whore, but Grant and I came up with the name Pendant Travel because of my necklaces.

We were not troubled by our disagreements or arguments because we were just trying to find our place in each other's lives, and we trusted each other. I made space for myself in his house, now our house, emptying one of the spare bedrooms to create my home office. I still used Streamline Travel as my host and I loved the fact that now Sara was not only my boss, but my soon to be sister-in-law.

Just after Teresa's beautiful snowy spring wedding, Teddy proposed to Sara.

Grant met everybody important to me and easily became a part of my family and circle of friends. Both Teddy and Rob joked around warning Grant about my special skill of knocking men down and even though Grant didn't believe it, I refused to show him. My days of knocking men down were behind me.

Grant and I decided on a small wedding ceremony at our home, inviting only close friends and family. His parents and sister came from New York to be a part of our special day, and the Paris trip was our honeymoon.

While merging my life with Grant's, I got a letter from the agency of my adopted family. The letter said that Michelle and her family no longer needed my help, and that the two-year commitment had been terminated by the receiving family. Tears filled my eyes—I was happy for her, but my heart ached because I felt like I was losing a part of my family. Then I saw a handwritten note from Michelle— she was still going to school, but she had a great job working in a dentist's office. She was finally able to stand on her own two feet and take care of her kids. She included her address, phone number and email address so that we could stay in touch. I was proud of her and happy to stay connected. Grant and I set up a college fund account for Samantha and Wesley, and we sponsored another single mother.

Looking back, I see that something bigger was at work while I had been suffering through divorce, loneliness and frustration about my life. I learned a lot about myself along the way, but not until I met a healthy man like Grant was I able to see my mistakes with men so clearly. After Nick and I divorced, I was scared. I didn't think any-body would love me, because I had stopped loving myself.

I believe I chose Sam because he had problems, too. Maybe that was our connection, two lost souls trying to escape our loneliness through sex. But now I can see that two needy people might create passion, but will never create a healthy relationship. Sam leaving me before the Cayman trip was a wonderful gift, even though I didn't realize it at the time. It was in the Cayman Islands that I began the process of letting go—letting go of my problems, mistakes and failures—and started to see that being alone wasn't so bad.

Meeting John was an important step along the road to becoming whole again. He helped me get past Sam and I started to feel hope about my future. But it was during that year while I was alone, before I met Grant, that I was finally able to enjoy my own company and get excited about my life with or without a man.

I'll never forget Sam or Nick or John because, like stepping stones, they helped me get to Grant. They helped me get to myself.

www.ingramcontent.com/pod-product-compliance
Lightning Source LLC
Chambersburg PA
CBHW021013180626
46814CB00003B/1269